SHADOW OF THE APOCALYPSE

(Joe Hawke #15)

Rob Jones

ISBN: 9798704427476

Other Books by Rob Jones

The Joe Hawke Series
The Vault of Poseidon (Joe Hawke #1)
Thunder God (Joe Hawke #2)
The Tomb of Eternity (Joe Hawke #3)
The Curse of Medusa (Joe Hawke #4)
Valhalla Gold (Joe Hawke #5)
The Aztec Prophecy (Joe Hawke #6)
The Secret of Atlantis (Joe Hawke #7)
The Lost City (Joe Hawke #8)
The Sword of Fire (Joe Hawke #9)
The King's Tomb (Joe Hawke #10)
Land of the Gods (Joe Hawke #11)
The Orpheus Legacy (Joe Hawke #12)
Hell's Inferno (Joe Hawke #13)
Day of the Dead (Joe Hawke #14)
Shadow of the Apocalypse (Joe Hawke #15)
Coming Soon: Gold Train (Joe Hawke #16)

The Hunter Files
The Atlantis Covenant (Hunter Files #1)
The Revelation Relic (Hunter Files #2)
Coming Soon: The Titanic Mystery (Hunter Files #3)

The Avalon Adventure Series
The Hunt for Shambhala (Avalon Adventure #1)
Treasure of Babylon (Avalon Adventure #2)
The Doomsday Cipher (Avalon Adventure #3)

The Operator
The Operator

A standalone action-thriller for fans of Jack Reacher and Jason Bourne

The Cairo Sloane Series
Plagues of the Seven Angels (Cairo Sloane #1)

The Raiders Series
The Raiders (The Raiders #1)

The Harry Bane Thriller Series
The Armageddon Protocol (A Harry Bane Thriller #1)

The DCI Jacob Mystery Series
The Fifth Grave (A DCI Jacob Mystery)
Angel of Death (A DCI Jacob Mystery)

Visit Rob on the links below for all the latest news and information:

Email: robjonesnovels@gmail.com
Twitter: @AuthorRobJones
Facebook: www.facebook.com/RobJonesNovels/
Website: www.robjonesnovels.com

CHAPTER ONE

Joe Hawke looked out of the helicopter window but saw only the black of night. Somewhere out in all that darkness, the northern Pacific Ocean raged in wild, unpredictable swells. Buffeted by the strong Kamchatka current, the chopper rocked in the sky. Hawke felt the same restless anger in his heart and readied himself for what he knew was going to be the most dangerous and savage mission of his long and challenging career.

The anger he felt was just the tip of the iceberg. The enemy he was soon to face and destroy had seized the White House in nothing less than a coup d'état and kidnapped one of his best friends, Alex Reeve, and her father, the true President of the United States. They had also put the entire ECHO team on the FBI's Most Wanted List and placed their leader, Sir Richard Eden under house arrest.

The degree of tension and rage he felt was matched only by his insane thirst for justice. But this went further than the personal. He felt a deep concern for the fates of millions of ordinary people who just wanted to live their lives. If a man like Davis Faulkner and his corrupt, depraved inner circle were left in power, it was those very same, innocent citizens who would suffer the most in the end. He had to stand up and fight not only for himself and his friends, but for every other man, woman and child who needed someone to look out for them, even if they didn't know it yet.

The black ocean below once again surged like a hungry beast and the Sud Aviation Frelon helicopter transporting Hawke and his team suddenly lurched to the right and began descending into the maelstrom. Knocked from his thoughts, he looked back through the window and saw a bright red parachute flare slowly descending over the sea. He made a quick assessment and gauged its altitude at around three hundred meters. He watched it slowly floating down toward the sea. Then, a gust of wind caught its tiny canopy and blew it out of sight to the east. Inches beside him, the raging wind thumped and clawed at the chopper's metal skin.

A second parachute flare started burning, again to their starboard. The small red light bobbed and jerked around in the wind as it floated on its parachute. The crew of the Japanese-registered Taihō Maru were sending the flares up to give the chopper pilot some improved visibility. Now, he brought the Frelon around ninety degrees starboard and descended further to the helipad on the rear deck.

Buffeted by yet more of the unforgiving Arctic wind as the blizzard raged through the Alaskan skies, the chopper felt like nothing more than a child's toy. Inside, the ECHO team held on for dear life as the cabin lights flickered on and off, increasing the sense of danger out in this remote wilderness. Hawke followed the trajectory of a third flare as it sank into the heaving sea, skimming across its frothing surface until a crest rose up and swallowed it down into the murky depths. The wild swell sucked and punched at the surface creating more crests and troughs several meters high. Then he saw a glimpse of their trawler, ploughing through the black sea and spraying huge arcs of foamy water either side of its broad steel bow.

Less than a day ago, they had been fighting Nikita Zamkov's army of AI robots in a rift valley deep in Antarctica. Just hours before that, they were engaged in lethal combat with thugs in Mexico City's most dangerous backstreets. Before this, a savage battle in the heart of the Amazon jungle. And before that, they'd had the fight of their lives against the notorious Congolese general and warlord known throughout the underworld as Joseph "King" Kashala.

When Hawke realized all of this had happened across the last few days of his life, he thought he was losing his mind. Could it really be true? Their lives moved so fast the answer was yes. It was true, and yes, he needed a good, long rest.

He turned from the window and glanced at the faces of his friends. No, that was wrong. The men and women surrounding him tonight were more than that; they were his family. Tonight, his family looked exhausted and battered but still up for a fight. Nikolai Petrov, the strange Russian monk and former Athanatoi cultist was at the end of the cabin on the opposite side. Tall, thin and almost ghostlike, he was trying to explain something to Kamala Banks with intricate hand gestures. The American Secret Service agent looked like she was following it well enough.

Lexi Zhang, the Chinese assassin and his lover long, long ago, was sitting back with her arms crossed over her chest and her eyes closed, but nodding to something Ezekiel Jones was telling her. The Texan tank commander seemed to be making a joke, but despite his own amusement, he raised not the ghost of a smile on Lexi's smooth, impassive face.

Business as usual there, Hawke thought. *I've been there, Zeke… Godspeed, soldier.*

Beside Zeke, Scarlet Sloane was finishing a cigarette with Vincent Reno. The former French Foreign Legion man was proud of his record of being able to smoke a filtered cigarette in less than forty seconds, but tonight he was taking things at a more leisurely pace. Twisting in his seat to face Cairo Sloane, he had his gnarled elbow resting on the bottom of one of the portholes and was listening carefully to her cut-glass words. When he laughed at something she said, Hawke saw her brush her neck and fiddle with her hair.

Surely, he thought, *it's only a matter of time before they get together, right?*

But after Camacho's death, she would need time to recover, first.

On his own side of the chopper, just to his left, Ryan Bale and Lea Donovan were also speaking quietly among themselves. The young geek he had first met all those years ago back on the streets of London had undergone a massive transformation but was still essentially the same intelligent and kind person he had always been. As for Lea, she was his fiancée now, which he found harder to believe than how much action they'd been through in the last few days. She represented full closure to his old life, his first marriage and everything that had come before ECHO.

Life.

And death.

He took a deep breath and gripped the rail above his head as the chopper increased its bank angle and corrected its hover pattern over the trawler. Landing on a ship in this weather was insane and they all knew it, but Orlando Sooke had assured them the pilot was the best in the business and regularly made trips out to ships in all conditions.

As a helicopter pilot himself, Hawke had enough faith to let the man get on with the job. He didn't envy him. Landing on a ship out at sea at night was as hard as it got. As the ship rolled in the darkness, the helipad on its stern deck yawed left and right as well as pitching back and forth while the entire ship heaved up and down in the sea. With all six movements to factor, plus fighting a severe crosswind, this was where a pilot earned his keep.

Hawke looked through the porthole once again and caught another glimpse of the ship. Wincing, he turned to his team. Noting the deterioration in conditions, he had lost confidence in a safe landing.

"No chance he's setting this bird down on that deck," he said.

"What, then?" Ryan asked.

He grinned. "I think you know what."

The pilot's voice crackled through their comms. "No landing tonight," he said. "Use the ropes."

CHAPTER TWO

Lea Donovan felt a sudden pang of nerves. She had rappelled out of helicopters many times before, even at night and at sea, so it wasn't this new development with the rappel ropes. It was something more. Something about this mission which was starting to get to her. Maybe she saw it on the faces of her friends around here, but maybe not. Perhaps it was just her. She felt broken and used up and ready to pack it all in.

Camacho's death had a lot to do with this, she knew, plus the relentless endurance course their lives had been recently. The ECHO team hadn't stopped for two weeks. After President Davis Faulkner's coup d'état and Jack Brooke's removal from the Oval Office, they had found themselves cut adrift and hunted as fugitives on the FBI Most Wanted List. Stalked by the notorious assassin Agent Cougar and picked off one by one as they completed the Orpheus Mission, they made their way to the Amazon jungle and then up to Mexico. There, they had taken out another ruthless enemy and finally flown from Uruguay up to Vancouver.

Lea struggled to accept all of this had happened in just over a week. She had never known anything like this whirlwind in her entire life and now, only hours after taking off from Silver City, the former Royal Canadian Air Force chopper, retasked as private transport helicopter, was coming to the end of its long flight after just one short stop on Kodiak Island for refueling.

"All ready to go?"

Hawke. He was on his feet now, sliding open the side door and lashing an abseiling rope to a handle inside the chopper. A sharp cold wind whipped sheets of rain inside the cabin. He looked at her and winked, feeding the rope out of the door and down toward the heaving deck. "Lovely day for a dip."

"Eh? You mean the great Josiah Hawke hasn't even got one poxy rope pun?"

"Afraid not."

She got up and walked over to him. "That's not even getting an eye roll."

"But how about a kiss?"

She kissed him on the cheek and slid on her backpack. "But only one, eejit."

"I'm touched," he said, moving his hand up to his heart. "Right here, where it counts."

"Get down the rope, you fool. We have friends to save and a President to put back in the Oval Office."

He grinned. "And I thought life in ECHO would be boring after the SBS."

Lea watched him go out into the night. When he hit the deck, she expected him to give her a thumbs up as the signal to follow. Instead, he moved his hand up to his heart again.

"Eejit," she said, and was second out after him, buffeted by the freezing winds as she climbed down the rope toward the ship's helipad. The deck continued to rise and fall beneath her with the surging swell, but Hawke was waiting for her with one of his arms holding him to a rail and the other one reaching out to her. She jumped the last few feet and crashed into him. He wrapped his free arm around her and pulled her tight into his body.

"I'm not in the mood right now, Joe."

"Funny girl."

They climbed rain-lashed steps to the docking bridge and watched as the rest of the team descended down the rope. When they were all safely on deck and making their way over to a position on the upper deck, the chopper turned in the night and was gone.

"Oh crap!" Hawke said as the team gathered around him.

"What's the problem?" Ryan called out.

"Yeah?" Lexi said. "What's up?"

He sighed. "We've only gone and landed on the wrong ship!"

Lea slapped his arm. "Damn it, Joe!"

"Sorry."

A man in a black oilskin raincoat and beanie appeared in the door behind Lea. "I'm Hansen, the captain of this vessel. I won't ask who you are," he said in a Norwegian accent, his voice thin and hoarse in the whining gale and horizontal rain. "I think the chances of you not being who we're expecting are low to zero."

They followed him inside the ship and he slammed the door. Instantly, the sound of the howling wind and rain was muted by the heavy steel. "Go down to the canteen and get some hot coffee. I'll join you on deck when you're finished."

"When does this insane storm end?" Scarlet asked.

"We're coming out of the worst of it now," he called back. "No more than another hour or two and things should settle down to merely uncomfortable."

"Excellent."

Inside the ship's mostly deserted canteen, they took off their Parka coats and gloves and packs and set them down against the bulkhead beside their table. The big Frenchman was already at the galley's small serving counter, balancing himself against the bulkhead as the trawler ploughed down another trough. "A very large pot of coffee and nine mugs, s'il vous plait."

"I'm surprised they're still serving hot drinks in these conditions," Kamala said.

When the men behind the counter had stopped laughing at her comment, Reaper staggered over to the table with the coffee pot and returned to the counter for some mugs. Gathered together at the table, Ryan spoke first. "Why not just fly the damn helicopter all the way to the island?"

"That's why we're on the trawler, Nimrod," Scarlet said. "You think you can just fly into Tartarus airspace in a bloody great chopper without getting seen on radar and shot out of the sky?"

"As you well know Cairo Sloane, I refuse to argue with you when it comes to bloody great choppers. Your experience is just too great."

"Certainly beats your lifelong experience of one tiny little chopper, darling."

He blew her a kiss. "Touché, but seriously, there must be a little isolated bay or something we could find to land in?"

"Maybe there is, maybe there isn't," Lea said. "The point is we don't know, so we can't take the risk. The island doesn't officially exist and it's not even on US military maps. We're lucky we know its location, never mind whether it has secluded places to come ashore without alerting the natives. Unfortunately, Orlando struggled to get us much information on the inner workings of Tartarus. It's one of the most secret bases in the US military. As far as we know, no one has ever got in or out of the place without official sanction."

"Until today," Hawke said. "Today we change all that."

"We sure do," she said.

"Just asking," Ryan said, turning and studying Lexi. "You seem very stressed."

"It's only natural," she said. "With Alex under arrest in Tartarus, you're the only tech nerd we've got on the team. This makes me both stressed and nervous."

He winked at her. "Thanks, Lex."

"Welcome, babe."

Nikolai looked at them and said deadpan, "So when are you two getting married?"

Hawke sipped his coffee and looked at the Russian monk. Nikolai was one of the team's newest members and usually best-known for his lack of humour. But every now and then, a rare quip or smile would escape from him. This was one of those times, and it was best to join in and enjoy it while it lasted. Soon, the thaw would ice over once again.

But serious or not, he was a good fighter. During the recent carnage in Antarctica, Mexico and the Amazon rainforest, Nikolai Petrov had proved himself to be a brave and hardened battler. Hawke was proud to fight alongside him, but he had his doubts he would stay in ECHO for very long. The young Russian was a loner and a deep-thinker. A philosopher. He needed time to process his thoughts and consider his place in the universe. As a man with a lot of leadership experience in the Royal Marines and the SBS, Hawke's best guess was Nikolai would soon be on his way.

"Wait a second," Kamala said. "If we know so little about the island, what exactly is the ingress plan?"

"I can answer that," Hawke said, sipping his coffee. "We're using an old SBS strategy."

"And what might that be?"

"We're going to make it up as we go along."

Reaper laughed and lit another roll-up. "Hilarious."

"The storm seems to be calming," Lea said. "That's good."

"Very good," said Zeke. "Because otherwise, using an underwater scooter is going to be like riding a bucking bull."

Ryan turned his head to Scarlet and opened his mouth, but she put her hand across his lips and scowled at him. "Say it and lose the balls. Clear?"

He nodded nervously. "Mm-hm…"

"Good work, soldier," she said with a smirk. "As you were."

Hawke laughed. "You're always best off avoiding insulting Cairo, Ryan. It might take time and patience, but this Mountie always gets her balls."

Scarlet raised a curious eyebrow. "And where would like your slap today, Major Hawke?"

"Give me time to think that over," he said with a grin.

She finished her coffee and winked at him. "Take as long as you like."

Hawke checked his old, scratched and battered diver's watch. Like many military men he had the face turned inward to minimise reflections in battle and enable him to see the time while holding a weapon without turning his wrist. "Refreshment time over. We need to get going to give us time to get ashore and get inland before daybreak. Alex and Jack are relying on us for everything. We can't let them down."

"Joe's right," Lea said. "If we screw this up, they're dead and it's the end of ECHO."

"So, no pressure then," said Ryan.

"No pressure at all," Hawke said. "Let's go and get our packs and equipment ready and get on with it. I'm not letting anything happen to Alex or Jack. Not ever." He got up and downed the rest of his coffee. There was no time for rest and relaxation now. The fuse was lit and burning down to the most dangerous ride of their lives.

CHAPTER THREE

When they stepped out onto the deck with their packs and weapons, the rain had moved further out to the east and the wind was slowing to a strong breeze. Cold, salty air whipped up off the surface on a spray of sea foam as they made their way down the listing trawler to the stern. Here, Captain Hansen was already overseeing the organization of nine Seabows. With over seventy-five minutes of battery power and a depth of forty meters, the powerful dual-motor underwater scooters packed more than enough punch to get the team members all the way to the southern shores of Tartarus.

Hansen looked at Hawke with sceptical eyes. “Are you sure you want to go through with this, Major?”

Hawke looked out over the rolling, gunmetal gray waves crashing over onto the surface of the freezing water. Tartarus was too far away to be seen and ahead of them, nothing but sea and air blurred until a misty, storm-lashed horizon.

“Why, you think it might be dangerous?” Hawke said with a grin.

“You could say that,” Hansen replied. “You can’t even see the island.”

“But I know how to read a compass, Captain, even an underwater one.”

“Don’t worry about us,” Lea said. “If we get into trouble we’ll hop on board Joe’s ego and radio for you to come and get us.”

Hansen’s stern face broke into a smile, then he laughed. “I guess you know what you’re doing, but I’ve been trawling these seas for decades. There’s no way in hell you'd get me going voluntarily overboard in any conditions, especially ones like we have today. Personally, I think you're all crazy."

"Being crazy is a prerequisite for joining our team, darling," Scarlet said. "If you weren't out of your mind you wouldn't last five minutes with us."

"All trawler captains who fish out here are *slightly* crazy," Hansen said, "but I can see this isn't enough to meet your requirements. I'll have to forget about joining you and settle for sailing back to port instead."

"Shame," she said with a shrug, slowly eyeing him up. "You'd have been good. I like the beard, too."

"Perhaps it's time for us to go," Lea said with a frown. "Whenever Cairo Sloane gets that look in her eyes, it's usually time for us to go."

After a nervous chuckle from everyone standing around on the deck, Hawke was first down into the icy water. Like the rest of the team, he had changed into a high quality neoprene cold-water wetsuit and was now securing his pack to a line attached to his waist as he bobbed up and down on the surface, already meters off the stern. There was no room for it on his back, because the space was taken up by a single scuba tank full of compressed air. The pack contained clothes and weapons, all waterproofed and ready to go.

Another pack splashed down in the water beside him. Then another and another. Moments later Reaper was crashing down into the sea, followed by Scarlet and Lea. When they were all in the water, Hawke saluted Hansen and called out to the team, focussing on Ryan, Nikolai and Kamala. "Remember, you're breathing compressed air from the tanks on your backs. Do not hold your breath at any point."

"Got it," Kamala said and Nikolai gave a thumbs up.

Ryan nodded.

Then, Hawke turned his Seabow to the north and pointed it down under the surface. Seconds later he was already ten meters beneath the waves and descending fast. For him, underwater was a home away from home, even in these conditions, but there were others on the team with much less experience. He slowed and looked over his shoulder.

Reaper was in visible range, and he could just make out Lea behind the Frenchman. The rest were out of sight, rubbed out from the world by the darkness of the underwater night, but the dive beacons attached to their wetsuits were clear enough. He counted the bright yellow lights in the murky gloom, and when the whole team were accounted for, he turned and checked his compass and resumed his course toward the island.

Time seemed to slow. The scooter's electric motor whirred in front of him and pulled him through the water. Minutes passed. Twenty, thirty… The current forced him to the east and required constant adjustment to steer back on course, much like flying into a crosswind. In the boredom, his mind drifted like the sea and he found himself thinking about his life.

His childhood and parents.

His father.

The Royal Marines. The SBS.

Liz, his first wife and her brutal murder. Was the sniper tracking and killing them today the same man who had killed his wife? His blood ran cold at thought of the killer's name.

Alfredo Lazaro.

He remembered the day his old CO, Commander Olivia Hart had first said that name to him in a briefing on Liz's murder. Known professionally as the Spider, Lazaro was a Cuban mercenary, initially thought to have been hired to kill him. At first, they thought the murder of his wife was an accident. Collateral damage. Lazaro screwing things up in Vietnam and hitting the wrong target. It didn't matter. Hart also told him that Thai Special Forces had taken Lazaro out in a raid on a strip club in Bangkok's Patpong District just days after the strike.

He held in the rage as the scooter pulled him across the ocean currents toward Tartarus.

Anger quickened his heart and stirred his soul not merely because his wife had been murdered by Lazaro but because she had been lying to him throughout their relationship. The woman he had believed was from southern England had been leading a double life. Elizabeth Compton's first name was really Elizaveta because her mother was not English but Russian. A spy from the western Russian city of Kaluga posing as an architect. She had traveled to the West as part of a Soviet trade delegation and it was in England she met Liz's father William Compton.

So many lies.

He fought back a wave of emotion as he remembered Maria Kurikova, a Russian spy who went on to join ECHO and have a relationship with Ryan. It was Maria who had broken the news of his wife's true identity to him, and how she had been a secret agent for MI6 and using her mother's KGB influence and contacts to turn FSB agents to work for the British. How her codename was Swallowtail and how Lazaro had been hired by the British Foreign Secretary James Matheson to assassinate *her* not him.

So many lies.

He checked the compass and made another adjustment.

The journey they had come through since those days had been long and bloody.

Olivia Hart was now dead, killed in action when her gun jammed, fighting the Thunder God's forces in the Emperor Qin's tomb in Xian.

Maria was also dead, cut down in her prime. Shot through the heart by the lethal sniper Ekel Kvashnin on the notorious Seastead Battle above Atlantis.

And he had personally executed James Matheson on his Scottish Highlands estate with the classic Mozambique drill – two rounds in the chest and a single shot in the center of his forehead. His fears circled back to Lazaro. If he really was the sniper taking them out one by one, there could be only one kind of payback and he would be the one to mete it out. For Liz, if for nothing else.

Hawke shook himself free of the ghosts that were gripping him and snapped back to the cold reality surrounding him. Yes, he had lost a lot of good friends on this journey but if he didn't keep his eye on the ball he would lose a lot more.

He tracked the seabed below as it gradually rose up out of the depths to meet him. The shore was approaching fast. He was sure they had stolen a march over the Tartarus authorities and would be able to make their way inland without alerting them. His plan was to reach some good, elevated ground and make a survey of the island. After that, it was back to making it up as he went along.

He was in shallow water now with the seabed less than ten feet below him. He cut the Seabow's motor and allowed his feet to sink down until he was standing on the sand. Then, he walked toward the shore until he was able to peer up over the surface and grab an eyeful of the view. His first glimpse of Tartarus was not reassuring. The beach was non-existent, and made mostly of jagged rocks. The wind drove waves of black water over them where they crashed into explosions of white foam.

He rocked in the water, sucked off his feet by a swell to his left. Righting himself, he pulled his pack along the line attached to his waist and began making his way toward one of the sharp black rocks along the shore. Selecting the easiest one, he climbed up out of the sea and scaled the rock until he was positioned out of sight from the shore and looking out to where his friends were about to surface.

He saw the beacons first. Then heads began to pop up out of the water. He waved his own dive beacon and alerted them to his new location. He counted them all as they climbed out of the sea and up the rocks with their packs and breathed a sigh of relief, especially when he saw Ryan, Nicolai and Kamala. They had made it through a perilous section of the mission all in one piece. Even though Ryan was more experienced than the other two, his confidence exceeded his ability and that made him more dangerous.

Scarlet was closest to him, scrambling nimbly over the rocks like a cat and releasing her breathing regulator from her face. "What now, Tarzan?"

Hawke turned and pulled himself up to the top of the jagged, sea-lashed rock. He scanned the shoreline and made a quick assessment of it. "We climb around this rock and then go over there to the east. That's the safest way onto the island. After that, we…"

"Yeah, yeah…" she said. "Make it up as we go along. I know."

He grinned. "You know me too well, Cairo."

She raised an eyebrow and looked him up and down. "I've certainly seen enough of you over the years, Hawke."

"But not as much as me," Lexi said, turning a mild smile on Hawke and placing her hand on his knee. "Remember Zambia, darling?"

"Easy tiger," Lea said. She was beside them now, slick-wet regulator in her hand and wiping seawater from her eyes. She raised her left hand and her engagement ring glinted in the soft light of Hawke's dive beacon. "Remember this, *darlings*?"

Scarlet laughed and began climbing the rocks. Lexi smiled and followed her, giving Lea a moment to scowl at Hawke. "What the hell was that?"

He opened his mouth to speak but she stopped him dead in his tracks with a long kiss. "And just you remember too, darling."

"No chance of forgetting," he said with a grin. "Let's get moving. I want everyone safe on shore and out of these wetsuits."

"Steady on," Scarlet called back over the rock. "I'm not that sort of girl."

"And into their *combat fatigues*, Cairo,' he shouted back. "Not naked."

"Thank heavens for small mercies," Ryan said. "I respect you, Cairo, but I think the elderly should be afforded a certain degree of respect in public."

Scarlet glanced down at his nether regions, tucked away behind his wetsuit. "Yeah, but it really would be a small mercy in your case."

"Hey!"

"C'mon," Hawke said, his grin fading fast in a flash of brief, broken moonlight. "To the shore and into our fighting gear. We have a long few hours ahead."

CHAPTER FOUR

What passed for a beach was nothing more than a grass-pocked dune twilight zone between the razor-sharp rocks of the southern coast and a thick forest of scrubby shore pines and Sitka spruce stretching into the prison island's interior. A good place to change into their kit, Hawke thought. They moved fast in the cold night and were soon in full fighting order.

Hawke made his way up a low rise and scouted around until he found what he was looking for – enough elevation and a break in the trees which gave him a view inland. Scanning ahead, he saw a ridge of jagged mountains covered in snow. A pale, faint glow emanated from some foothills to the east. On an island entirely uninhabited except for the military base where they kept the prisoners, this could mean only one thing – he had found the compound where they were keeping Alex and Jack.

He turned to walk back down into the forest when from out of nowhere, a black silhouette appeared in a gap in the trees. The figure moved fast, raising a hand in the air and rushing toward him. The night was too cloudy for constant moonlight, but he still saw something glint in the man's hand and knew it was a dagger.

He stepped into the fight, pulling a combat knife from his holster with one hand while using the other to block the other dagger. The man was strong. He batted away Hawke's blocking arm and drove his blade up toward his stomach, aiming for just under the ribs. Hawke struggled to dodge the attack, slipping on broken pinecones littering the forest floor.

Then he saw another figure, and a third. Dressed in black combat fatigues and wearing beanies, the men moved without speaking. Fast and efficient, they emerged from the trees like ghosts, each armed with the same blades.

These guys are good, he thought. But how did they know we're here?

A pinecone crunched behind him and he turned to see another man approaching from the south. That made four on one, he considered – unless he got really lucky and more were on the way. He grabbed the fourth man's arm and pulled him close, ramming his knife up into his ribcage and smashing his elbow into his face. The assailant grunted in pain, but the crash of surf against the black rocks drowned out his cries. He collapsed to the forest floor dead and Hawke kicked him away before turning back on the other three.

They rushed him all at once. Hawke thrust his blade out and caught the arm of the man on his right. He cried out in shock and lost his focus. It was all Hawke needed. He grabbed his wrist, rotated it around hard until the bones crunched like a packet of chips and then yanked him down to the ground. As he sailed past him, Hawke slashed the blade across his throat and killed him.

One of the other men slashed his blade at him, nearly sending him falling back over the dead man behind him. Hawke struggled to right himself, arms windmilling for a few seconds and leaving his chest and throat area vulnerable. The other man took advantage, lunging forward and thrusting his dagger into Hawke's throat.

Hawke worked with what he had, and let himself fall back over the man. Better that than a knife in the throat. Anticipating the fall, he twisted in the air and hit the ground rolling. Scrambling to his feet, his boots crunched on the dead twigs and cones as he turned to face the assailants once more. He caught a glimpse of one of the men's faces. Camo grease hid all detail but he was older and had the calm, focussed eye of a seasoned Special Forces pro.

No surprises there, Hawke thought. If Tartarus really were one of the most secret locations in the US military, they wouldn't be using boy scouts to guard it. Other things had already given them away. The way they moved, coordinated and with no talking and straight to business – all of this was the hallmark of the best.

The older man rushed him again. Hawke leaped back to avoid his blade, actually feeling the razor-sharp tip of the serrated combat knife rip open the front of his fatigues. Close, but no cigar. With the man's knife at arm's length, he quickly brought the handle of his own blade down and struck his wrist with the heavy steel pommel.

The man grunted and released the knife. As it thumped on the ground, Hawke wanted to move in for the kill but now the other man attacked from his right. The former SBS man threw himself into a forward roll and sprang to his feet behind the first man, who was still disarmed. Hawke acted fast, spinning his knife around throwing it at the second man. The blade spun through the air like a shuriken star and buried itself into his throat, dropping him instantly.

The first man crouched down to pick up his knife but Hawke was faster. He snatched up the blade and twisted around onto his back, hooking the man's feet out from under him and sending him tumbling forward. Hawke held the dagger out and he fell on top of it, his substantial weight grinding the thick, sharp blade deep inside his guts.

Hawke pushed the dead man away from him and scrambled once again to his feet. Pulling his combat knife from the other man's throat, he wiped his blood off on the dead man's fatigues and checked for any sign of other assailants. Sensing no one else around, and presuming the guards worked on a four-man detail, he sheathed his knife and jogged down the rise back toward the shoreline.

He saw Lea first, standing apart from the others and looking up into the trees. When she saw him, he saw her shoulders slope down slightly in relief. As he crunched over the bracken and dunes, the rest of the team saw him and walked over to Lea.

"Why were you so long?" Lea asked.

"You want the good news or the bad news?" he said.

"The good news, I think."

"I know which compass heading we need to get to the compound."

Scarlet picked up her pack and shouldered it. "And the bad news?"

"We've got company."

"What sort of company?' Ryan asked, peering over Hawke's shoulder.

"Dangerous company. Four men, all armed with combat knives. They rushed me up there on the rise just to the north of those rocks. We all expected the compound to be heavily guarded, but now we know the entire island is, so everyone on their best behavior, please. We don't want to let ourselves down tonight."

"Joe's right," Lea said. "Keep your eyes peeled at all times. They could be anywhere."

"And we need to be somewhere else," Hawke said. "Namely, rescuing Alex and Jack. They need us more than ever and we're their only hope."

"That's if they're still alive," Scarlet said sombrely.

"They're still alive," said Hawke. "Now, let's go get 'em."

CHAPTER FIVE

Alex Reeve sat alone in the darkness, staring at her wheelchair with a deep, burning resentment she hadn't felt in a long time. Her mind tortured her with the memories of when the Athanatoi's mysterious elixir had given her back the use of her legs.

She had walked and run alongside the rest of her teammates through the Medusa, Valhalla and Aztec Prophecy missions. By the time they were battling against Dragan Korać to discover the secret of Atlantis, the elixir had faded and she was once again confined to the wheelchair.

What had been inside that mesmerizing liquid? If she closed her eyes she could still see its strange golden glow even now. The way it sparkled and fizzed like it was electric. What had the immortals known about life and longevity? How had they harnessed the elixir to live so long, when the ECHO team had only been able to use it to give her back the power of walking for such a fleeting time?

Her mind now drifted to ECHO.

When was the last time she had even seen the rest of the ECHO team? They were searching for the Land of the Gods when she and her father were arrested and imprisoned. That was over a week ago. Or was it closer to two weeks? Keeping track of time in a dark cell with no clocks wasn't an easy business.

She pulled herself up on her elbows until her back was pressed up against the cold concrete wall and breathed out a long, deep breath. As if all of this wasn't bad enough, she still had her father to think about. That psycho Davis

Faulkner had said he wanted some kind of show trial for him, but what if something had changed his mind?

What if circumstances had changed the game and now former President Jack Brooke needed simply to disappear? It didn't bear thinking about. If they killed him, she would also be killed. Both wiped out in this God-forsaken hellhole and no way for her mother and the rest of the world ever to know the truth. She felt tears welling in her eyes and wiped them away, cursing her weakness. Locked away in here, her mind was as useless as her legs.

And where the hell was Joe Hawke?

Truth was, she had fallen in love with Hawke the first time she met him, not that she ever had a chance to tell him. Now, those feelings were subsiding, forced out of her mind by the reality of the world. He was engaged to Lea. They would get married on some beautiful Irish beach and have about ten kids. She saw it all unfold in her mind in a picture-perfect, soft-focus dreamland.

No resentment. She loved them both. They were the best friends she had ever known. Good for them. But it didn't make it any easier to think about. Would she even be alive when any of that happened? Was Hawke on his way to save her?

She sunk back down into the uncomfortable bed and pushed her head down onto the thin foam pillow. Closing her eyes, she let out another long sigh and hoped her father was still alive and that help was on the way. Hope, it turned out, was now the only thing she had left in the world.

*

Jack Brooke was asleep when they came. The heavy steel door swung open and let a greasy yellow light into his cell. How many times had he danced this waltz? Two soldiers marched into the cell, one armed with an assault rifle. The other man wore a holstered pistol and two corporal stripes.

"Get up," the corporal said.

Brooke had not seen this one before. This interested him because he guessed he had maybe underestimated the size of the compound. Then again, maybe the shifts rotated from another base somewhere more often than he had thought.

"I asked for my breakfast call at seven," he said. "And seeing neither of you has any fresh orange juice or eggs, I'm going to say no."

The man with the assault rifle stepped further into the cell and turned the weapon on him.

"I said get up, old man," the corporal repeated.

"Hey, I'm not that old. I know when my birthday was."

"And now you know when your deathday is, too," said the man with the rifle.

The corporal scowled at him. "Shut up, Tanner!"

"Sorry, Corporal!"

Brooke furrowed his brow and swung his long legs off the bed. "What the hell did he just say?"

"He said nothing." The corporal grabbed a fistful of his shirt and pulled him to his feet with a sneer on his face. "Nothing at all."

"It sure didn't sound like nothing to me, son. I want to speak with Colonel Blanchard."

"Well, that sure is a coincidence," the corporal said. "Because Colonel Blanchard wants to speak to you, too."

Grabbing hold of his shoulder, the corporal spun Brooke around and slapped some cuffs on him. Then he navigated him out of the cell and into the bright lights of the corridor. After so long in the dark, Brooke squinted to give his eyes more time to adjust as the armed men marched him across to Blanchard's office. The truth was, now he was nervous. He had heard precisely what the young soldier had said back in the cell and it didn't take a genius to interpret what he had meant by it.

So, Faulkner had decided to take him out of the game permanently.

It was an outrage against decency and honour and democracy, to be sure, but he knew that wasn't anything Davis Faulkner couldn't square with his degenerate conscience. Would the people ever know the truth of what happened here on this island? He doubted it. The American people didn't even know about the island. He knew from his experience in the Oval Office that keeping a secret from billions of people wasn't as hard as some might think.

After they had done the deed and murdered him, his body could be flown anywhere and any story could be constructed. He guessed a depressed suicide was at the top of the list. He had lived a good, honorable life. Served in the military and built a distinguished career there. Risen to the highest office in the land and served the people honestly as their President. To end like this was a crime that only future historians would truly understand and yet he could accept his death if it meant going with dignity.

But Alex.

As far as he was concerned, his daughter was untouchable. If any of the vermin on this island tried to kill her, he would do whatever it took to save her and damn his dignity. But would doing whatever it took be enough, out here in this hellscape? What resistance could he possibly offer? Maybe Faulkner was bluffing. Yeah, that was it. The son of a bitch was stewing down in the Oval Office and was upping the ante to try and get him to confess. That had to be it.

Didn't it?

CHAPTER SIX

Hawke led the way back up the rise and through the small clearing where the four dead soldiers were sprawled out among the pinecones. From here, he was able to point out the faint shimmer of light he had seen earlier before the men had attacked him.

"We won't always be able to see it," he said. "Not when we get down into some of the valleys among the trees, so set your compasses now to thirty degrees. Everyone do it, please. If we get separated we'll meet up just south of the compound."

As everyone set their compasses, Hawke spied the easiest way down off the rise and into the forest ahead of them. "That's our way in."

Kamala drank some water from her canteen. "Seems easy enough."

"For now, but it's going to get harder," Hawke said. "Those foothills are much higher and steeper than they look, plus now we know we're not alone."

Ryan looked down at the corpses. "We sure do."

Hawke moved first, navigating his way down off the rise and sweeping rogue pinecones out of the way wherever he could to clear the way for those behind him. The rest of the team followed him in single-file and made their way off the rise and into the dense spruce forest. In here, the icy sea wind was filtered by the tall trees and the temperature rose several degrees.

"That's better," Lexi said. "Finally out of that wind."

"Unless Ryan eats his full ration of beans before we get to the compound," Scarlet said. "Then we're all in for a nasty surprise."

"Just like any man who goes back to your bedroom," Ryan said.

Zeke laughed. "Nice return of serve, my man. Very nice."

"Give me a right of reply, at least!" said Scarlet.

She had no chance. A bullet traced past Hawke's face and buried itself in the trunk of one of the Sitka spruces a few feet away. "Down!" he called out, and threw himself to the forest floor. "That was an inch away from blowing my face off."

"Which direction?" Lea said.

"West," Reaper said. "I felt it too, but it didn't get as close to me as it did to Joe."

They scrambled to the east side of some nearby spruce trunks and drew their weapons. Lea was scanning the darkness but saw nothing. Beside her, Scarlet was already fitting a pair of night vision goggles to her head.

"Where are they?" Lea asked.

"Nowhere near," came the reply. "No heat signatures anywhere near us."

Reaper said, "Then it looks like we have a sniper."

"Not the same one who's been tracking us?" Ryan said in disbelief. "How can he know where we are?"

"Depends who's pulling the strings," Scarlet said. "If it's Uncle Sam, working out we'd be coming up here to rescue our friends isn't exactly the most vexing deduction to make."

"It's just a hunch, but I don't think it's our old friend," Hawke said.

Lea glanced over at him and saw his face partially obscured by the darkness. "What makes you say that?"

"He missed."

"Joe's right," Nikolai said. "Not once has our old friend, as he puts it, missed the first shot."

Scarlet scanned a brief glimpse of the mountain ridge just visible through a break in the trees off to their right. "I see him now. His head just peered over some boulders on the side of the mountain right above the compound.

Hawke got to his knees and pressed himself up against the trunk. Poking his head out, he looked over to the ridge. "Makes sense. Yeah, I see the little bastard. Now we know where he is, we can stay out of his line of fire."

"He's too far away to see us, but he must have a mighty good pair of magnified night vision goggles," said Scarlet. "Especially considering we know he has some friends wandering around down here on the lookout for us. He's not going to want to take any of them out by accident."

"What's he doing now?" Ryan asked.

"Funnily enough," Scarlet said, "he's put his gun down and is giving us a cheery wave."

"You're kidding!"

"Yes, I'm kidding, idiot. What do you think he's doing? He's got his weapon sighted on our current position and he's waiting for us to make a move."

"Then let's not disappoint him," said Hawke.

"Are you nuts?" Zeke said.

"I think maybe he's losing it," Nikolai said. "It can happen when a man ages."

"Less of that, you cheeky bastard," said Hawke. "If you cut the gags and look over to my right, you'll see another way through the trees that descends quite sharply down into a valley."

"I see it," Lea said, already preparing to move.

"Down there, we'll be out of the line of fire, and our man up on the ridge can't shoot around bends or down into valleys. Ready for the off?"

Kamala started to ask something but he was already gone, breaking out of the cover of the wide spruce trunk and tracking across to a slope leading down to the valley. The sniper fired instantly and the bullet traced past his head and buried itself into the trunk of another pine behind him. But he was too fast, weaving in and out of the trunks until safely down in the initial section of the valley.

"Who's next?" he called out. "See if you can beat my time."

"I'll go," Lea said, sarcastically. "I feel an uncontrollable urge to be with my man."

"Attagirl!"

Reaper was already on his feet, but still crouching down behind the trunk he had used for cover. "I'll fire a few rounds in his direction while the rest of you go across the clearing. This will give him something else to think about and maybe damage his aim."

When Lea was halfway across the clearing, Ryan scrambled to his feet and followed in her tracks. Kamala and Nikolai were next, each taking different paths to confuse the shooter. Then Zeke and Lexi made the same move, heads down and sprinting across the scrubby clearing.

Lexi's path took her further to the north where her way was blocked by a fallen, thunderstruck Sitka spruce. No problem. She leapt into the air and crested the burnt trunk like a deer before crashing back down to earth in a hail of sniper rounds. The bullet chewed into the trunk and ricocheted into the ground beside it. With bullets blasting dead wood and mud and pinecones all around her, she tucked herself into a dive and rolled the rest of the way out of the clearing.

"Don't think he likes you very much," Ryan said.

"I don't think he likes any of us," said the Chinese assassin, dusting herself down and scowling at him.

Ryan grinned in the darkness. “No, but *you* I think he liked even less than the rest of us.”

Lexi opened her mouth to let him have it when Scarlet and Reaper came thundering out of the clearing in a second wave of sniper fire and narrowly avoided a collision with them.

“All good?” Hawke said.

“All good, Chief!” called Zeke.

“Then let’s get moving,” Hawke said. “The sniper knows our position on the grid and he’ll already be in contact with our beanie-wearing friends to let them know where we are. The sooner we get going, the better. We go to the east first, before turning north.”

“Why?’ Kamala asked.

“Same reason we did it in the Amazon Jungle,” Hawke said. “If they know where we are and where we want to go, they can set up a welcoming committee for us somewhere along the way.”

“Ah… I’m with you.”

“Boobytraps, ambushes, you name it,” Hawke said. “And judging from past experience, I don’t think the people on this island are very nice at all. In fact, I’m starting to doubt if they’re even going to offer us tea and biscuits when we get to the compound.”

Lea rolled her eyes in the darkness, but gave his arm a squeeze. “What a lovely idiot I’m marrying.”

“Don’t worry Lea,” Ryan said. “I once read in a science journal that children generally inherit their intelligence from their mother.”

“Thank God for that,” Hawke said. “Now let’s get going. We have a long hike and one hell of a fight at the end of it.”

CHAPTER SEVEN

Through the night, they marched. No paths anymore, just forcing their way through the dense pine forest and stumbling here and there over fallen cones and branches. Ryan thought he heard something growling in the distance – some kind of big cat, maybe. Reaper was sure he saw something on four legs leap from a boulder behind them. Scarlet used her night vision in the trickier sections but wanted to keep the batteries fresh for the assault; they had zero doubts that when they made their move the lights would go out.

Then, rotors.

Still at the head of the line alongside Scarlet, Hawke raised his hand and gave the signal for the team to halt. He turned to Scarlet. "You hear that?"

"I'm standing right next to you, Joe," she said in her typical, withering fashion. "Of course I sodding well heard it. But it's not a chopper."

"And believe me, that's an expert's opinion," said Ryan's voice from back in the line. "If anyone knows her choppers, that someone is Cairo Sloane."

Scarlet pursed her lips. "That joke wasn't funny the first time you said it, or the fifty thousand times you said if after that."

He chuckled. "Sorry, I'll think of a new way to insult you. Promise."

"It's getting closer," Lea said. "Must be a drone."

"This is what I think, *aussi*," Reaper said. "Maybe very close to the tops of the trees."

"All ready to get a nice picture of us for the mantelpiece," said Lea.

"Or fire something nasty at us," Hawke said. "Remember Hell's Inferno?"

The whirring sound of the tiny rotors drew louder as it closed in on them.

"So, what do we do?" Kamala asked.

"Sounds like there's only one of them," said Hawke. "We should get under the sleeping bags in our packs. They're made of foil."

"Will that be enough to save us?" Nikolai asked.

"For sure." Ryan let his pack slide off his back and began to rummage around for the foil sleeping mattress rolled up in a tight bundle at the side. "Aluminium foil is electrically conductive. It will easily destroy any attempt by infrared to locate us down here on the forest floor."

Hawke already had a hold of his mattress. "Just unfurl them and then lie down and pull the mattress over you, foil side up. It's way too dark down here for a regular light camera to pick us up and as the man here says, the foil's electrical conductivity means killing their little IR party before it starts."

He pulled the thin mattress up over his body and ensured he was fully covered by it. The drone was almost over them now, and sounded like it was being flown up and down the forest inside some sort of grid formation. Made sense, he thought. They had probably already flown up and down the section between the compound and where the sniper had sighted then. Now they were working their way out in systematic grids until they located them and then the good ole beanie boys would be redirected to take them out before they got anywhere close to HQ.

Yeah, good luck with that, he thought.

High above the pine tops, the sound of the rotors receded into the night.

"You think they saw us?" Zeke asked.

“No chance,” said Hawke.

“Could you guys keep it down,” Ryan said with a yawn. “I’m trying to get some sleep here.”

Scarlet was already on her feet, packing her foil mattress away into her bag. “Get up, boy. We’re still a long way from home.”

They moved on, and the next hour passed in almost total silence. Like the rest of the team, Hawke was scanning the forest for any sign of trouble, but even with sporadic use of the night vision they saw nothing but trees and rocks. Then, they finally reached the barren, hostile slopes at the base of the mountain. Much closer than before, their new position was too low to give them a view of the compound, but they knew it was up there somewhere.

After the long and dangerous hike, Hawke took a second out to slow his breathing and study the rockface in front of them. As with so many missions, the easy ascent was also the obvious one. That was why he had navigated the team further to the east where the climb was much more dangerous, but less obvious.

“You can’t be serious?” said Lexi, staring up at the rockface. “You think I’m Spiderwoman or something?”

“I’d need to see you in brightly colored spandex before making that call,” said Ryan.

Lexi gave him her middle finger.

Hawke was still staring up at the rockface. “This way we keep the element of surprise.”

“Sure we do,” Lexi said. “Because they know no one would be insane enough to approach the compound from this direction. I like your logic.”

“Are you sure you’re not making this up as you go along, Joe?” Kamala asked.

“Does no one listen to my briefings?” said Hawke. “Of course I’m making it up as I go along!”

Nikolai looked unhappy. "Courageous. Insane, of course, but also courageous."

Hawke slapped him on the back. "The way I see it, mate, is this. If even *I* don't know what I'm going to do next, how does the enemy?" After the stunned silence, the ex-marine lowered his pack to the ground. "We go up without the packs, and the last man standing down here will tie them to a line and we'll hoist them up. We need our gear but we're not going up a rockface like this with them on our backs."

They followed his orders and readied their climbing equipment. Moments later, the harnesses, chalk, ropes, carabiners, quickdraws and hammers were all ready and to hand. Hawke took the first step, and took one last look at the rockface. Harder than usual but easier than the one they had climbed in the Amazon Jungle.

The Aleutian Islands were a string of pearls stretching across the Bering Sea from eastern Russia all the way across to Alaska. They were at the Alaskan end tonight, where the North American tectonic plate met the Pacific tectonic plate, forming a large subduction zone. The resulting geological mayhem had caused molten rock to bubble up to the surface and create over forty active volcanoes, otherwise known at the Aleutian Islands. This gave him some idea of the sort of rock the mountain was made of. He coated his hands in chalk, shouldered a number of robust, nylon climbing ropes and reached up to the first hold.

"Wait," Kamala said. "What do we do if we're halfway up the rockface and the drone comes back?"

Hawke considered the question. "Standard operating procedure is to freeze like a rabbit in some headlights."

"But what if it starts shooting at us?"

"Again, normal procedure is to get shot in the back and fall back to earth, landing like a bag of strawberry jam on the rocks below."

She crossed her arms and glared at him. "If you mean strawberry jelly, I don't think that's very funny."

"Either jam or jelly describes what happens if you fall two hundred feet onto rocks," he said with a smile. "So pay attention to my holds and when I get to the top I'll lower some lines."

She shook her head and covered her hands in chalk. "Crazy English bastard."

CHAPTER EIGHT

After a short break on a ledge halfway up that he had spied from the ground, Hawke made his way up the rest of the rockface slowly and methodically. Mountain climbing was about patience and consideration as much as it was about strength and courage.

He had secured a number of pitons into suitable crags and splits in the rockface to provide anchors and attached quickdraws to their eye holes through which he had threaded his line as he made his way up. This would protect him if he slipped and fell and also gave the rest of the team a trail to follow up the rockface.

He resumed the ascent, inserting each piton and hammering them into carefully selected rock fissures. Letting himself down with sloppy judgement was one thing, but killing a friend because of it was quite another. Satisfied, he attached the quickdraw and threaded the rope through it and then made his way onto the next one.

Inch by inch, he felt his way up the ancient rockface. Icy wind whipped off the sea behind him and chilled his bones as he worked slowly up the mountain. Nearing the top now, he began to feel the effort of the ascent in his fingers and hands and shoulders. The storm-scarred ocean heaved and raged against the craggy coast behind him. Ahead, an unknown number of heavily armed and well-trained soldiers guarded an illegally imprisoned president and his daughter.

This is what is was all about, he thought. No matter what has happened or is about to happen, there is always a single, specific moment in time somewhere in life where everything pivots. Sometimes it could be boiled down to just a few seconds. This was one of those times, wild and dangerous. All the hell they had been put through by Faulkner was now behind this moment. All the amazing new adventures they had yet to discover and experience were ahead of this moment.

He finally reached the top and stopped just shy of the edge of the rockface. Tucked into the cover of some craggy boulders, on a broad ledge near the top, he was finally able to see the glow of the compound above him. He heard a truck engine grumbling somewhere off to his right and then some men shouting. Had they seen him? No. They started laughing and then the truck moved away.

Turning, he saw the pine forest and then beyond it, the wild, surging sea stretching away into darkness. The Taihō Maru had never been in sight of the island, so there was little point looking for it. He peered over the edge of the rockface and saw his friends far below. Speaking into his palm mic, he told them the coast was clear and they began making their way up.

Lea was first up and was soon sitting beside him checking her weapons and retying her hair into a tighter ponytail. Ryan and Scarlet followed and then the rest of the team except Reaper were all on the ledge. He had stayed below to attach all the packs to the lines.

Hawke spoke in a low whisper. "Depending on wind direction, you can hear the voices of the guards every now and again. I've also heard a couple of trucks driving up and down. I'd say we're less than fifty feet away from some sort of gatehouse. Get your weapons ready while I check that out."

He crept up the last few feet of rock and peered over the edge of the rockface. He was right. There was a substantial gatehouse less than fifty feet away to the east, badly tarnished by the corrosive effect of the bitter climate. He could see at least four soldiers standing in front of it. They looked bored and cold. There were probably more inside. Two had rifles and the other two had sidearms in holsters. The road he had heard the trucks driving on meandered away down a gentle slope to the west before bending out of sight as it twisted north again. He guessed it was one of several vehicular access points to a compound of this size and importance. He also presumed there would be helipads and maybe even a runway or a submarine docking station carved deep inside the mountain. It all depended on just how many people they wanted coming and out of here without the rest of the world knowing about it, including covert satellite reconnaissance from other states like Russia and China.

He climbed back down to the ledge and reported what he had observed. In his absence, the team had pulled their packs up and Reaper was now climbing up onto the ledge. After a short rest, they got their strength back and readied their weapons. It was still the dead of night and dawn would come slowly to this part of the world so they had darkness on their side, for now at least.

"C'mon," he said. "We all know what we have to do."

As he moved to leave, Lea stopped him.

"What is it?" he asked.

"You really think Alex and Jack are still alive?"

"Damn straight I do," he said. "Nothing else is worth thinking. Let's go get them."

Hawke moved fast, pulling himself up over the top of the rockface and bracing for the fight of his life. He had known it was coming for a long time now, and now it was here, right up in his face. Right here on Tartarus.

CHAPTER NINE

Over the edge of the rockface and into the jaws of death. As they advanced on the enemy, the four soldiers at the gatehouse turned into eight in a heartbeat. Not the end of the world, Hawke thought. He and the rest of ECHO made nine soldiers and this wasn't exactly their first fight.

Not by a long shot.

The soldiers armed with rifles pulled them up into firing position while the men with pistols flipped open their holsters and reached for their weapons. One of the men pulled a radio from a utility belt and started to speak. Hawke instantly knew he was already their biggest problem and raised his gun into the aim.

Another soldier screamed and told them to freeze and drop their weapons. Another ordered the soldiers to open fire on them. Some fanned out into defensive positions. The chaos was ended when Hawke fired on the man with the radio and shot him in the head, killing him instantly. This was the point all confusion was cleared up once and for all.

The remaining soldiers fell back into a defensive position behind Jeeps and trucks and opened fire on them with a raging fury driven by the lethal shot that had taken out one of their own. Hawke had no need to order his team into cover in response to the assault; they had already made themselves safe. Some had tucked down behind other vehicles parked up on the side of the road opposite the gatehouse, others led by Lea had arced around to the east and were using the rear of the gatehouse itself as cover.

Hawke took out another soldier with three shots to his chest and threw himself into a rolling dive to avoid the brutal fusillade raining down on him in reply. He ended up crashing into the back of a giant metal bin of road salt. It made good cover and gave him time to survey the battleground one more time.

It now looked like there had been no more than eight soldiers manning the gatehouse and four of them were already down and out. Three at his hands and one right now, shot through the head by Reaper as he tried to scramble from his cover behind a Jeep back to the gatehouse. Hawke guessed they had gotten lucky and the soldiers needed to get back into the gatehouse to reach a radio and warn the rest of the base.

Too bad, he thought.

You're not going to get even half a chance.

Rounds pinged off the salt bin, He ducked his head down into his shoulders instinctively and tried to figure out who was taking pot shots at him. By his count, there were only four soldiers left alive after the latest exchange of fire. Two were behind a filthy mud-splattered MACK dump truck and another had positioned himself behind a concrete road divider splitting the road just in front of the gatehouse. Where was the fourth?

Another bullet ricocheted off the salt bin and none of the men he had just spotted were the one firing on him. He heard a heavy exchange of fire at the back of the gatehouse and looked up to see Lea and her team shooting at the men behind the MACK. They were making their way around the north side of the building to come in around behind the soldiers on their exposed side.

It was smart work, but not enough. The only way the soldiers could get away from the attack and maintain some kind of cover was to move around to the other side of the MACK, which exposed them to Hawke's position behind the salt bin. The soldier behind the concrete divider tried to fend them off, but Hawke was watching him closely. As he crawled forward to take another shot at Lea, Hawke fired on him and shot him through the face. It was ugly, but the seasoned SBS man didn't flinch. The son of a bitch was shooting at his fiancée, after all.

Now, the two soldiers taking cover behind the MACK were in a bind. They decided to split up, but this was a big mistake. Lea took out the one on her side of the truck and Hawke was able to shoot the other as he tried to take cover behind his side of the MACK.

Good work, but it still left the mystery shooter.

The last soldier fired on him again. This time Hawke saw sparks on the bevelled edge of the salt bin as the bullet pinged off into the night. Judging by the position and direction of the sparks, he knew the shooter must be somewhere further to the west than he had thought. Swivelling around on his ankles and raising his gun, he scanned the road leading away from the gatehouse and finally saw his man.

He must have been one of the soldiers taking cover behind the MACK truck who broke away and then got isolated. Now he was trapped between the devil and the deep blue sea, behind a jumble of rocks on a gentle rise to the left of the road. On one side, the rockface and the other the ECHO team and a bloody heap of dead colleagues.

Hawke raised his gun to take him out but was a second too late. Just as he was about to squeeze the trigger, the top of the man's skull blew off and he tumbled backwards behind the rock. He might even have gone right over the rockface, but Hawke had no way of seeing. What he did see was Scarlet Sloane strolling across the parking lot outside the gatehouse. She slid her gun into her holster and leapt over the corpse by the concrete divider and then made her way over to the salt bin. The others soon followed.

She looked at Hawke and then over to where she had killed the last soldier. "What took you so long, darling? I thought you were trying to let him kill you."

"I was about to shoot him," he said, holstering his gun. "But then I remembered how much you like killing men so I thought I'd leave it to you."

"You mean you need to go to Specsavers, darling. How old are you, exactly?"

"Funny. If you can bear to suspend your hilarious jokes for a few seconds, we have a gatehouse to search."

"What are we looking for?" Kamala asked.

"Radios, maps, delicious chocolate bars," Hawke said.

"And vodka," Scarlet said, the cold wind whipping her hair. "It's a small hope, but it burns nonetheless."

"Hold that thought," Hawke said. "And follow me."

CHAPTER TEN

It was little consolation, but Jack Brooke thought Blanchard looked uncomfortable with what was happening. He looked like a man who had bitten off a hell of a lot more than he could chew and was starting to regret it. He guessed a man like him must be corrupt to have been put in this place by Faulkner, but he still looked out of his depth. As the big old USAF Colonel occupied his desk like a burned-out CEO, the corporal and soldier who had dragged him from the cell were standing at ease behind him, either side of the door, armed, locked and loaded.

"I hear you're going to murder me tonight," Brooke said calmly.

A long pause, then Blanchard pulled a cigar from a wooden box and offered one to his prisoner. "From one military man to another, sir, I'm only following orders."

Brooke waved the cigars away and sneered. "Assholes always use that excuse, Colonel. I expected better from you."

"Orders from the very top, sir."

"Davis Faulkner?"

Blanchard hesitated, then lit the cigar. "I guess present circumstances mean I can talk about it now."

"You mean because I'll be dead before morning?"

"Long before that," Blanchard said with a glance at his watch. "Truth is, there's a team of terrorists on the island right now conducting some kind of operation to rescue you. I informed the White House the moment I had the intel and President Faulkner immediately ordered your execution. He cannot and will not let you fall into enemy hands. This is a serious business, sir. Nothing goes higher."

Brooke felt his pulse quicken on hearing about the rescue team. Maybe a splinter group from inside the US military. He was former US Army, after all, and Faulkner was very unpopular with the military. But more likely, he thought, it would be ECHO, that crazy bunch of international former Special Forces and nerds and monks and comrades-in-arms who had taken his daughter into their fold and treated her like family. Even helped her walk again. Now they were risking their lives in this hellhole to save him and his girl and restore him to the presidency.

Maybe.

"I can see that puts you in a very tight position," he said to Blanchard.

The colonel frowned. "How so?"

"Because if it's who I think it is, the team on this island is the best on Earth, Colonel Blanchard. They *will* save me and my daughter. When they do, you can count on them taking a very dim view of what you have done to me and Alex on this island."

Blanchard shifted uneasily in his seat and sucked on the cigar. Blowing out a long column of fragrant blue smoke, he tightened his shoulders and grew tenser. "They won't save you, sir. No one has ever successfully infiltrated Tartarus, despite many daring attempts in the past to rescue various terrorists and political defectors being held here. No one has ever escaped, either."

"And where is this team now?"

"I don't suppose there's any harm in my telling you. They're around one of the gatehouses."

"Too bad."

"For them, sure. They have no idea what hell is about to rain down on them. Like I said, you have no way out of here. Even if you do get off the island, and we both know that's impossible, but let's just say hell freezes over and you do, you can't touch Faulkner. He has a ring of steel around him. If you get through that, he has a dead man's switch. You go anywhere near him and he'll bring Armageddon to the United States. It's a scorched earth policy. A real classic."

Brooke could hardly believe what he was hearing. "And yet apparently, you still think he's the good guy and I'm the terrorist."

Blanchard curled his lip. "I *know* you're a terrorist, Jack. I know you were involved with ECHO and we all know they were behind the devastating terror attack in Hawaii." A long pause. "Like I said, there is no hope here for you. This is Tartarus."

Brooke played it calm. Blanchard had already said there was a team *on the island.* That alone was a major success in the rescue mission but he didn't want to get cocky. An old-time poker player, he considered he maybe had a full house right now, but what did Faulkner have? Four of a kind? A straight flush? Maybe a royal flush; there was no way to know. Not yet. He decided some old-school bluffing was in order.

"They *will* save me, Colonel. If it's ECHO, and I'm guessing Faulkner has already briefed you on ECHO, then this is the end for you, even if you kill me first. But if you turn over to my side, they'll play nice and let you live. Maybe you could be part of the vanguard against Faulkner and his corrupt regime in Washington."

Blanchard just sat and smoked his cigar, quiet and impassive but with that look of discomfort in his weary eyes. Too much risk. A hard-earned pension down the drain. Maybe even taking a bullet. "President Faulkner is strongly of the view that *you* are the traitor, Mr Brooke. I took another briefing from his Chief of Staff just a few hours ago on your activities with ECHO and I have to say, I think you're skating on thin ice right now if you're trying to recruit me to act against a sitting president alongside an international terror group."

"If you believe anything that asshole Josh Muston says, then you deserve everything that's coming to you. He's no more than a monkey on a string attached to Faulkner's chair leg."

"A charming image, but he's also a very-well briefed and senior White House official with the latest, highest quality military and CIA intel. Word is, you're a traitor, and tonight you're going to try and escape from this facility. But Faulkner has no need to worry about any threat you might pose."

"No?"

"No. Turns out you're going to take a weapon from one of the guards – using your extensive military experience – and in the attempt to discharge that firearm in a bid to escape, you get shot dead by guards."

Brooke bristled at the calm, nonchalant way he spoke. "Is that so?"

"Yes, sir."

"And my daughter?"

Blanchard paled slightly and took another long draw on the cigar. He rolled the thick smoke in his mouth before puffing it out into the air between them. "I'm sorry to inform you that she gets killed in the crossfire."

Brooke leapt from his chair and lunged at Blanchard. "You son of a bitch! You go anywhere near her and I swear I'll..."

He felt two sets of big hands grab him from behind and pull him off the desk. The soldier spun him around and pinned his arms behind his back and the corporal pounded him in the stomach repeatedly, beating the air out of his lungs and badly winding him.

"Enough!" Blanchard yelled.

The corporal stopped the beating. When the soldier released Brooke, the former president fell down to his hands and knees and strained and gasped to heave some air back into his lungs.

"That wasn't very clever, Jack," Blanchard said.

Brooke was still too winded to talk, still straining and heaving with a big close-up of Blanchard's threadbare rug and the corporal's boots in his face.

"You think I want this?" Blanchard said, stubbing out his cigar in a big, thick glass ashtray on the edge of his desk. "You think I like doing this? I'm a soldier, damn it. The President of the United States is my commander-in-chief and he just gave me direct orders to kill you and your daughter and that's what I'm going to do! You men! Get him up!"

"Sir!"

Blanchard fixed his gaze on the corporal. "Send two guards to the daughter's room. They have to be in the same place when the shooting starts for the story to hold together."

"Sir!"

As they wrenched Brooke to his feet, the former president now stared deep into the eyes of Colonel Blanchard. "Last chance, Blanchard! Are you with me or against me?"

Blanchard straightened his uniform out and swiped his officer's cap off the desk. Slipping it on his head, he ignored Brooke and stared at the corporal. "Get him out of here now! Take them down to the cells. That's where this is going down."

CHAPTER ELEVEN

The nine comrades in arms searched the gatehouse and quickly located some spare ammo and a map of the island pinned to the wall in the back room. Tattered and yellowed with dirt marks all over it from years of use, it wasn't the major breakthrough they were hoping for. While the main outline of the base was reproduced to scale, most of the internal sections were unnamed. Only the canteen and other general areas were specifically listed.

"For obvious reasons," Hawke said, turning to a disappointed team. "This is about as much use as a chocolate teacup. These alpha-numeric designations could mean anything – M3, G7, E12. Anything at all."

"No wait," Lea said, pointing on the map to something resembling a small square with a cross through it. "What is this symbol here? And another here – what do you think they mean?"

"Wait, I know!" Ryan said. "They mean you shouldn't put this map in a dishwasher."

"Stop talking, Bale," Scarlet said. "Immediately."

Ryan shrugged. "Just trying to help, Cairo."

"And you can best do that by shutting your yap."

Ryan gave Scarlet a salute. "Consider it done."

"Getting back to these symbols," Lea said. "Any idea?"

"They don't indicate corridors," Hawke said. "If you look closely, you can see they all seem to be in the middle of rooms."

"I hear something," Reaper said.

They stopped, and then they all heard the sound of a chopper approaching from the main compound, north of their position.

Reaper ran to one of the gatehouse's windows and scanned the sky. "Apache," he said, grimly. "Armed to the teeth and coming in this direction."

"Damn it," Scarlet said. "They know we're here. Maybe one of the guards got a message out."

"Or maybe a hidden CCTV," said Zeke. "That's more likely."

"It doesn't matter what sent them here," Hawke said. "All that matters is that they are here, and that chose to arrive in a helicopter gunship."

"Don't worry about it." Ryan waved his pistol in the air. "I'm totally sure we can defend ourselves against hellfire missiles and hydra rockets with these popguns."

Outside, the metallic whomping sound of the aircraft's four-blade rotor and mean growl of its General Electric turboshaft engine grew loud enough it almost shook the gatehouse.

"We might not have to," Hawke said. "I think the squares on the map represent access points to a tunnel system running beneath the compound."

"Either that or they're just the location of air-conditioning vents," Zeke said.

"They're not," Hawke said, pointing to the ceiling. "You see an air-conditioning vent in that ceiling?"

"I do not."

"And yet there's a crossed square clearly marked in the corner of this room right behind that filing cabinet."

Lea's eyes brightened with hope. "Which means…"

Hawke smiled. "We need to move the filing cabinet."

"Guys, the Apache! It wants to play with us," said Reaper. "It's descending down to ground level."

"Quickly into the tunnel!" Hawke said. "It's going to strafe us!"

He wrenched the filing cabinet out of the way and tipped it over. It landed with a crash on the wooden floor and revealed what he had been hoping to see – a trapdoor with a recessed steel handle fitted on it.

"You were right," Scarlet said. "Will wonders never cease?"

Hawke grabbed the handle and pulled the trapdoor open. At the exact same time, the chopper swung around and lined up with the main window at their backs.

"Into the tunnel, now!" he yelled.

Kamala and Nikolai were first, dropping down into the shaft and disappearing into the darkness below. The rest of the team followed, leaving Lea and Hawke up top when the Apache opened fire and began strafing the wooden gatehouse with its M230 chain gun.

With thirty-mil rounds tearing the hut to pieces, Hawke roughly shoved Lea into the tunnel and she tumbled inside. As the walls exploded all around him and a giant fireball ignited in the air, he threw himself down behind her and crashed arms-first inside the narrow shaft. He threw himself into a rolling dive and then sprang up to his feet, only yards from the chaos exploding behind him.

"Go!" he yelled.

But they were already on their way, sprinting down the tunnel. He ran after them, now just inches ahead of a wall of fire and smoke chasing him down the tunnel. Above, the sounds of the chain gun stopped and then he heard a missile roar away from one of the Apache's wing pylons and rip into what was left of the gatehouse. A deep, terrifying explosion thundered and growled above their heads as the air-to-ground missile blasted the gatehouse into a million pieces of matchwood and splinters and charred metal.

"You okay?" Lea asked when he caught them up.

"Sure," Hawke said. "But I'm not sure that was a great way to blow a $115,000 missile."

"Yeah," drawled Scarlet. "Will no one think of the taxpayer?"

"We need to keep going," said Hawke, with a sly glance at his old SAS friend. "They now know our location and they'll send much more after us to stop us getting inside."

"But which way?" Nikolai said.

Hawke looked around. As the smoke from the explosion above cleared, he saw they were standing in the tunnel system's equivalent of a junction box. Six concrete corridors went off into the darkness in various different directions. No signs, no indications of where they led and only a low, green emergency light illuminating the way.

"At least we have the lights," Ryan said.

The lights switched off.

"Idiot." Scarlet cuffed him around the back of the head. "You just had to say it."

"Night vision on," Hawke said, rummaging around in his now badly charred and crushed backpack. "They know we're down here so they've cut the lights and they're going to send soldiers down after us."

"But which way?" Kamala asked.

"This way," Hawke said, pointing at the corridor ahead of them.

"How do you know that's the right way?" Lea asked.

"I don't, exactly," he said with a shrug. "But the walls have more scuff marks on them than the other tunnels so I'm guessing it's used more than the others."

"This is why I'm marrying you."

"Aww," Lexi said. "Now shut up and get moving!"

Hawke was already ahead of them, pounding down the dark concrete corridor with a gun in his hand. The green glow of the night vision goggles might be strange to some on the team but not to him. His previous existence in the military had made him accustomed to them and he moved forward as fast and as sure as if it were broad daylight.

"Anything ahead, Joe?" Lea said through the comms.

"I see a door," was the instant reply. "I'm putting charges on it. Everyone stand back."

Lea looked on through the night vision goggles as Hawke fitted plastic explosives to the door and then ushered everyone back. When he detonated the C4, the explosion wrenched the door clean off its hinges and revealed a large, low lit room. Not much was visible. All metal, including some stairs leading up to another door on the far wall. Then the sound of boots on steel, men screaming and guns being readied.

"Get ready everyone," Hawke said. "It's going down."

Then the soldiers emerged through the door at the top of the stairs. Some of them were holding rifles, others handguns. They were all wearing combat fatigues. USAF, junior ranks by the looks of it. Maybe some Marines in there, but no way to tell. Shafts of green electric light shone through the corridor door as the soldiers filled the room.

A young corporal screamed at the soldiers. "Smoke 'em! Smoke 'em all!"

And then the battle began.

CHAPTER TWELVE

"Dad? What's wrong?"

Alex knew her father well enough to know something was seriously wrong. Seconds ago she had been locked in her cell in the darkness. This is what her life had been for so many days or weeks she had lost count. Then, the penetrating lights in the ceiling had flickered angrily on and the heavy metal door swung open to reveal her grim-faced father and a number of soldiers. They were so well-armed she thought they were about to invade a small island somewhere. Standing beside them, Colonel Blanchard the base commander also looked uneasy.

"Get into the chair," Blanchard said. "You're coming with us."

"What's going on, Dad?" she said, totally blanking Blanchard.

Brooke's face was a study of agony and indecision. He was fighting something deep inside himself, unsure what to tell her, but she already knew.

"You sick bastards," she said.

"They're not going to harm you, darling," Brooke said, struggling aggressively in the soldiers' iron grip. "I won't let them lay a finger on you!"

"Keep it down, Jack," Blanchard said. "You want to upset the other inmates?"

"What, you're afraid they might find out about your being a homicidal maniac who murders innocent young women in wheelchairs? I bet your family would be really proud of you right now, you sick son of a bitch."

The soldiers bristled at the insult to their commanding officer, but Blanchard waved them down. "I'm a military man, Jack, and these are military orders. You are a terrorist and a danger to the vital national security of the United States."

"I'm the democratically elected President of the United States, and you are taking part in a coup orchestrated by Davis Faulkner. You're making a big mistake."

Blanchard almost grinned. "What are you trying to say, Jack?"

"I'm saying that if I survive this, you will not."

Blanchard paled a little but quickly regained his composure, for his men, if nothing else. If he didn't have their confidence, he had nothing. "I hope you're not trying to scare me, Jack. I gotta say, I don't scare easily."

"That remains to be seen."

"If that's a threat, it failed to reach its target," Blanchard said. "I already told you what's going down tonight. You're checking out, and your friends have failed. They're too late. Even if they decide to get their revenge and take down President Faulkner, they'll still fail."

"That's right, the little ring of steel you talked about. Care to expand on that?"

Blanchard was now grinning fully. "You know what curiosity did to the cat, right?"

"What's the matter, frightened I'm going to make it after all? I thought you said I was checking out tonight? I guess not, if you're too scared to tell me what Faulkner's little plan is."

"Not scared at all. It's national security."

Brooke laughed loudly. "Now I've heard it all. A colonel telling the president he can't discuss national security."

"A *former* president."

"That also remains to be seen."

Blanchard sighed. "It's over, Jack. You have minutes to live. If your friends try and take on the president, they're going to get millions of people nuked."

"What?"

Inside the cell, Alex was moving too slowly. Two of the soldiers marched into her cell and grabbed her, roughly manhandling her over to the chair.

"Take your filthy hands off her!" Brooke yelled.

"Easy, Jack," Blanchard said. "Let's not make this any harder than it has to be."

Brooke calmed down. Focused. "Are you all right, Alex?"

She nodded, tears in her eyes. Let down and scared. Where was Hawke?

"What the hell did you mean by saying *nuked*, Blanchard?" Brooke said.

"Three nuclear bombs, each situated in a city inside the US. A ring of steel around the presidency. A scorched earth policy. If ECHO go anywhere near the president, he'll set them off and bring the Apocalypse to America, killing millions and blaming ECHO for the whole thing."

"My God, I knew you were corrupt but this is on another level. And I knew Faulkner was out of his mind, but this is beyond evil."

"Nothing will happen to anyone, so long as your little team stand down. It's that simple."

Brooke looked confused. "I don't understand how Faulkner could even get weapons like that out of the official stockpile and avoid serious scrutiny."

"They're off the books," Blanchard said. "Stored here on Tartarus. Have been for years, along with their deactivation codes and the men who flew out and installed them." He puffed out his chest. "The president put me personally in charge of the operation."

Brooke was almost speechless. "Where are these weapons?"

Now, Blanchard laughed. "It's over, Jack. And it's time to go."

"You can't do this, Blanchard!" Jack yelled.

"I can and I have." He turned to address the corporal. "Let's do it."

*

In the cell beside Alex's, a young woman shut her eyes and tried to blank it all out. She had heard the shouting and screaming outside in the corridor. Words floating in the darkness, some blocked by men talking over each other and some blocked by the cold steel walls of her own private universe.

Maybe this is how it ended for all the prisoners on Tartarus, she wondered. Maybe they were only kept alive for some sick experiment before being taken out to some cold, black snow-filled yard somewhere and shot through the head. But isn't that what happened in murky, violent dictatorships? She couldn't bring herself to believe it might happen in her own country. Something else must be going on.

Word among the inmates was that the former American President Jack Brooke was locked up here, but she had never seen him. Or his daughter, whom she had also heard was a prisoner behind these high steel walls and razor wire fences. When someone told her in the exercise yard one freezing snow-blasted afternoon, she had dismissed it as total garbage. Prisons were full of stuff like this – loose talk and casual lies and false hope and broken dreams and brittle desperation.

And she would know – most of her life had been spent in and out of US county jails and state penitentiaries.

More accurately, most of her life had been spent *busting out* of US jails and state penitentiaries. Nowhere had ever been able to hold her, until this. Until Tartarus. For the first time in her life, she had officially given up hope, and not just of escaping. She had even given up hoping she might ever see her boyfriend Ravi ever again. He too was behind these walls somewhere, but Blanchard had kept them segregated from the day of their arrival. No words, no shared smiles, no kisses.

Bastard.

Did one of the soldiers out in the corridor just say the name Jack? She could have sworn up and down that she just heard the name Jack. And so damn what? No one knew how many inmates were held on the island, but however many, there must be more than a few Jacks locked away here.

Right?

But then, what was the screaming and yelling for? Inmates were all locked away at this time of night and any screaming in the cells was rapidly and harshly dealt with. Hardwood cudgels and steel truncheons and pepper spray. She had been beaten more times than she could remember and even hosed down with icy water in her first few weeks. She guessed Ravi had taken worse thanks to his fighting spirit and defiance.

There it was again.

Jack.

And now she heard a young woman pleading. Could it be that Jack Brooke and his daughter Alex really *were* being held on Tartarus after all? She couldn't imagine why that might be; she'd had no access to any kind of news for so long she could barely remember how to read, and this meant she had no idea about what was happening in the world. Last time she had any freedom, President

Brooke was a hero war veteran and one of the most populate presidents in modern times.

Just how the hell could he end up in a place like this?

But she wanted to believe.

When she finally broke out of here, that would make heads turn back on Ehukai Beach. Kahlia Keahi in the same prison as President Jack Brooke, maybe even on the same block. From surfer gang to sharing the same roof as the president in a few short years.

Imagine that.

She leaned back until her head was touching the cold concrete wall and sighed. Maybe she might embellish it a little. Maybe the president really *was* locked up here and she got to know him. Walked in the yard with him, shared a table in the canteen with him, got to know his daughter. She guessed the daughter had to be a pretty stuck-up little bitch, but still, they could be friends, at least when she was telling the story back on her favorite beach with a cold beer in her hand and her gang family all around her.

She smiled at the thought, but the sound of more screams and then gunfire startled her from her daydreams. The scream was a woman's, and close. The president's daughter, maybe? She didn't even know her name. But the gunfire sounded much further away – not from outside in the corridor with the voices. Wherever it was coming from, it sounded like it was sending shockwaves through the men outside her cell in the corridor. They screamed and yelled and scrambled to action.

She didn't know what, but something was going down here tonight.

Something big.

CHAPTER THIRTEEN

Hawke led the team into battle. Reaper was first, storming through the door into the center of the steel room, batting soldiers out of the way and raising his gun into the aim. He fired at soldiers rapidly and without mercy. Bullets ripped through muscles and flesh and shattered bone, killing several of them in seconds and sending their bodies crumpling to a floor already littered with the dead.

The soldiers scrambled for cover behind crates and boxes and under the stairs. Blood gushed and pumped from the dead, dying and wounded as the wired French legionnaire searched for another target. He saw a flash of metal in the corner of his eye and flicked his head to see a soldier standing above him on the metal balcony in front of the other door. He was older and holding a handgun. An officer, maybe.

Reaper fired and blasted the gun from his hand but the officer's reaction was lightning. He pulled a knife and now the blade was reflecting the green glow of the emergency lighting.

Reaper's reaction was even faster. He levelled his gun and fired on the man at the same moment he threw the blade. The officer collapsed to the floor with a bullet in his face as the knife spun toward Reaper's head. He yanked his head back and to the side with a fraction of a second to spare as the spinning, serrated blade flashed past and smacked into the steel wall behind him.

Another soldier ran into view behind the dead man. He was moving fast and with deadly purpose. He vaulted the mesh fencing and drew his gun while he was still airborne. Reaper was pumped and reacted fast. He raised his gun and fired at the man, breaking his lower leg open and shattering his shin.

The man screamed and fired on him, missing by inches, then crashed into the riveted floor in a heap and reached for his leg, howling in pain. Reaper fired at him and struck him twice in the head, permanently ending his misery and pain.

Chaos. Another gun flashed to his right. Another soldier screamed in pain and the lights flickered on and off. Zeke was rolling down the metal steps, disarmed and disoriented. Kamala was running through the smoky, blood-soaked bedlam to him, trying to snatch up the gun Zeke's assailant had knocked out of his hand. Hawke and Scarlet were engaged in hand to hand combat behind him. Lea was firing on the balcony from behind the cover of an electrical utility box. More guards appeared and rushed toward Zeke and Kamala, but Reaper was already engaged in battle with a heavy-set soldier who had burst through a fire door a few feet away to his right.

The man was armed with a US Marine Corp Ka-Bar. The famous fighting utility knife had been used by the Corps since World War Two and never bettered. This was with good reason, but Reaper had fought with them and against them many times. A firm believer that you should never bring a knife to a gunfight, the Frenchman raised his pistol and fired on the man. Nothing happened except a dry click.

In the bloody mayhem he had miscounted his remaining rounds. No time to curse. He tossed the gun and reached for his own combat knife, a trustworthy workhorse of a steel blade complete with solid wooden handle and blood grooves. Cashing out at nearly eight inches long, the blade felt like an extension of his arm.

The Ka-bar slashed at his face but he was ready, ducking and sidestepping. It flashed through the air to his right so close that he heard the metallic hissing noise as the razor-sharp steel sliced through the air. He lunged forward and knocked the soldier's knife arm away, bringing his own blade up into his stomach. Aiming for the ribcage and driving the blade's tip forward with all his might, the attack failed when the soldier saw it coming and threw himself backwards.

Dodging the blade by inches, he had a second to regroup. Then, he lunged forward and fired his head forward into Reaper's face. The Frenchman flicked his head to the left, narrowly avoiding a broken nose and a lot of pain, then returned the compliment. Grabbing the soldier by his right shoulder, he launched his own headbutt. He was faster and heavier and bang on target and his thick forehead made short work of the man's nose, smashing it to pulp and spreading it all over his face.

As the soldier crumpled unconscious to the floor, Reaper scanned the brawling chaos in the room and saw a corporal on the steps, screaming orders and raising his gun to take a pot shot at one of the ECHO team. Reaper didn't follow the aim and see who the target was – it didn't matter. All that mattered was that he stopped him before he squeezed the trigger and wasted one of his friends in this hellhole.

Reaper sprinted across the floor, leaping over dead bodies as he went. He reached the balcony in seconds and grabbed the rail. He was tired and knew he was going to ache like hell in the morning, but right now the adrenaline pumping through his veins drove him on like a demon.

Grabbing the rail, he pulled himself up over onto the balcony with all his remaining strength and charged down the narrow steel walkway toward the red-faced corporal. He smacked he gun out of his hand and punched him in the jaw in one fluid movement, spinning the younger man around like a top and sending him crashing to the floor.

Then, he kicked his gun away and gave him another hefty punch to the head, knocking him out and hefted him over the balcony.

"Blimey Reap," Scarlet yelled across the room, ducking a punch. "You threw him in there like a side of beef!"

He shrugged. "Admit it, you're impressed by my muscular physique and stamina."

Pleased with his work, he scanned the room for his next challenge but saw only a grenade spinning through the smoke toward his face. No time to think, he threw himself away from the lethal projectile and prayed he had gotten far enough away. Still flying through the air, the grenade detonated right behind him and blasted him with the shockwave. He cradled his head as the force of the blast powered him into the steel wall beside the stairs but it was too late.

The shockwave was too strong and drove him hard into the wall. He saw it coming but had no time to react, and then his world went black.

CHAPTER FOURTEEN

Hawke was a few short yards from Reaper when the grenade exploded and blasted his friend up into the air. Shielding his face from the debris and with the chaos still raging all around him, he watched the Frenchman fly across the balcony in a cloud of smoke and flames. He crashed into the wall and slid down to the floor. Was he dead? No, moments later he regained consciousness and staggered to his feet, angrier than ever.

That was Vincent Reno. Taking a non-lethal grenade shockwave direct to his body and being knocked out and just shaking it off to return to battle. He'd never once doubted the Frenchman's strength of character, loyalty or physical resilience and this just compounded the great respect he held for his old friend. The old legionnaire scanned for another fight, found a young soldier reloading a gun in the corner and made his move.

Hawke left him to it. Through the mayhem and screams, the former Commando heard a heavy man pounding along the floor behind him. He spun around and saw a red-faced corporal was suddenly inches away. Up close he looked slightly older and more jaded, and Hawke saw a scar running along his chin. It looked like a bayonet scar, telling him this man had seen close-quarter action. The corporal was gripping his combat knife in his hand and didn't waste time introducing himself.

He came at Hawke fast with the blade. He was too close for Hawke to respond with an offensive move, so he sidestepped the lunge and let the screaming soldier slice through the air to his left. With the knife still in mid-arc,

Hawke now reacted, lunging forward, blocking the knife arm with his left hand and punching the soldier hard in the stomach with his right hand.

He heard a rib crack and the pain shattered the soldier's angry face. Hawke gave no quarter, now spinning fast and hooking the other man's legs out from under him. As he tipped over, Hawke finished the job by swinging his right elbow hard into the man's left temple, smashing him out cold.

Scarlet ran over to him, stepping on the unconscious soldier as she approached. "That was the last one, Joe. They're all out of the game now."

"All except the men guarding Jack and Alex," he said.

Lea ran over, some blood on her cheek.

"Are you okay?" Hawke asked.

"Sure," she said. "You should see the other guys."

He chuckled. "Good work."

"Which way do we go now?" Kamala asked.

Hawke looked at the door the soldiers had burst through. "Smart money's on that way. C'mon!"

They sprinted up the metal steps and along the balcony and then stepped through the door, reloading guns and raising them into the aim. Another long corridor awaited them, but this time the bare concrete walls and metal fittings were replaced by white painted walls and CCTV cameras up on the ceiling.

"Looks like we're finally inside the main prison," Lea said.

They ran along the corridor, shooting out CCTV cameras as they advanced deeper into the notorious black site. After what seemed like forever inside the winding labyrinth, but was only a few minutes, Hawke turned a corner in a long corridor and finally found what they had come for.

"Gotcha." Hawke saw Alex first; at least he saw the glint of the overhead strip-lights on the spokes of her wheelchair. Then he saw the woman inside it, holding her face in horror as she was looking at something just out of his sight around another corner. The corridor was lined with chunky steel doors on both sides and he guessed this was one of the main areas where the prisoners were held.

"Follow me," he said quietly. They made their way up the corridor, Alex still in sight but unaware of their presence. He walked wide to the other side of the corridor to get a better look around the corner. Then he saw it.

Two men in military fatigues were holding Jack Brooke against his will, gripping him like iron and forcing him to turn away from another military man holding an assault rifle up into the aim. Hawke knew immediately what was going on. They were trying to shoot Jack Brooke through the back and make it look like an escape attempt.

Seeing how Alex was being made to watch her father's execution, and knowing she would be next, raised the temperature of his blood to boiling point. So, this was what the Faulkner regime looked like out in the field.

He pulled back around the corner, out of sight of the men and readied his weapon.

"What is it?" Lea asked.

To their horror, Hawke explained. "And we're totally out of time."

Scarlet was champing at the bit to get into another fight. "How many men? How many?"

"Does it matter?" Ryan said with a sleazy smirk. "I heard you can only take three at a time."

She grabbed his balls and twisted and stifled his scream with her hand. "You're not too old to put over my knee, Bale. So, keep going and I'll fill you in, you little wankspangle."

His eyes widened, but Hawke pushed her away. "Enough. In answer to your question, there are six of them, all armed with assault rifles, and what looks like the base commander. Colonel insignia and a sidearm on a belt. I'm going in. You back me up with some seriously nasty cover fire."

"Wait!" Lea said, her voice low and desperate.

She and Scarlet had seen the button at the same time. A dirty red palm-sized button covered in the grease of a thousand jailers' hands. Written above it in red capitals was a small plastic sign: EMERGENCY CELL DOOR RELEASE.

"Let's make things interesting, shall we darling?" Scarlet said.

"But that's so naughty," Lea said with a wink.

"My sentiments exactly. At least it will give the guards something else to think about and increase our chances of escaping with Jack and Alex."

Lea smacked the button down. "Done!"

"Hey! I wanted to do it."

"You snooze, you lose, babe."

Scarlet gave her a wry smile as the sound of a loud warning klaxon and a dozen steel jail cell doors sliding open filled the air.

"Nice," the two women said together, sharing a high five.

Blanchard heard the siren and started. "Find out what's going on!" he shouted at a soldier. As the young man snapped to attention, Blanchard turned to Brooke and raised his gun at his head. "Goodbye Jack!"

Hawke spun around the corner, his gun raised at arms' length. "I don't think so."

Blanchard turned in horror but never got a chance to register what had happened. Hawke fired three shots into his forehead and another two in his chest, dropping the big man like an old moose. His fleshy body crunched down onto the hard linoleum tiling and blood sprayed out of his head and chest all over the white floor.

Brooke had reacted like a ninja, spinning around, crouching down and dashing toward his daughter the second he heard the gunshots. The soldiers reacted a heartbeat later, turning and aiming their guns at Hawke. And Lea, Scarlet, Reaper, Ryan and the others. The rest of the team had now piled around the corner and opened fire with a vengeance, aiming high to miss any chance of striking Brooke and Alex.

Hawke dived into a forward roll and came to a stop beside the dead base commander's body, raising his gun. The nearest soldier tried to swing around with his assault rifle but the corridor outside the cells was cramped and he struggled to lift the gun into a good aim. Good. Hawke had counted on it, and now he fired into the man's forehead and killed him on the spot.

He crashed to the ground with a heavy thump and more blood sprayed out over the white walls and floor. Hawke scrambled over to Brooke, who was already behind the wheelchair and running as fast as he could away from the close-quarter battle unfolding in the corridor. He stopped en route and snatched up Blanchard's personal weapon, an M9 handgun and checked it was loaded.

"Glad to see you, Hawke," he said calmly.

"You too, sir, and you Alex."

"Hey, Joe! Damn, am I happy to see you!"

As Nikolai shot the last of the soldiers, Hawke smiled. "Me too." He turned to Lea and Scarlet, his smile fading. "Go back along the corridor we just came down and make sure they're all dead and that we're not being followed. We don't want to get taken out in a pincer attack."

"On it," Lea said. "C'mon Reap, Ry."

"So, what's the plan?" Brooke said, then seeing Hawke's reaction, he sighed. "Don't tell me, you're just making it up as you go along?"

"Me? Never!"

On cue, several prisoners spilled out of the cells. Others turned the corner ahead of them, all armed with anything they could get their hands on – fire extinguishers, chair legs, one was even holding a shattered light bulb by its steel screw cap. It looked nasty, but not as nasty as the look on the prisoner's face.

Hawke was surprised to see a young woman among them, covered in tattoos. Hands, arms, neck and much of her face. Now, she sprinted over to them, holding a handmade shank in her hand made from what looked like the metal from some sort of plumbing pipe. He raised his gun and aimed it at her.

"Take it easy, we're the ones who let you out."

The woman ignored him and stared at Jack Brooke, her mouth falling open. "Damn, the rumors were true. You're President Brooke."

"I am, and we're in trouble. Can you help us?"

She turned her frown on him. "I think not..." She looked at the other men, one of them a little longer than the others. He had dark black hair and two dark green eyes set in a confident but tired face. He mouthed something in a foreign language to her and then she nodded.

"All right, maybe we can. But only if you help us."

"Meaning?" Hawke asked.

"You're not here to break the president out of his prison cell to take him on a picnic out in the snow, right? You're here to get him off the island. You get me and my friends off the island and you've got yourself some help."

Hawke and Brooke exchanged a look. "Is that going to be possible?" asked Brooke.

"Depends on what kind of plane I can steal to get us off the island," Hawke said.

"Then it's possible," the man said in a Brazilian accent. "There are plenty of transport aircraft here, down in the hangars."

"But they're heavily guarded," said the woman.

"Then there's nothing to debate," Brooke said, turning to the tattooed woman and smiling at her. "You have a deal."

Lea sprinted around the corner, shocked to see the armed prisoners. "Whoa. That worked quicker than I thought."

Scarlet and the others joined her, breathing hard. Raising her voice to be heard over the klaxon, Scarlet said, "They're all dead, Joe, but we saw more running down the corridor behind us. We should make tracks."

"Agreed," Hawke turned to the tattooed woman. "Can you get us to the hangar?"

"Sure," she said. "Just follow me. I'm Kahlia, by the way."

"And my name is Hawke."

"Joe Hawke," said Ryan. "Licence to kill."

The woman scrunched up her face. "Huh?"

"Wait," Brooke said. "I can't go into detail right now, but Blanchard told me about a major national security threat to the United States. One orchestrated by Faulkner."

"The VP?" Kahlia said

"He's President now," Brooke said with disgust. "And very dangerous."

"What did he tell you?" Lea asked.

"Like I said," Brooke said, looking at the prisoners, "I can't go into detail. This is Top Secret stuff. Let's just say it involves nuclear weapons and deactivation codes, which I know are on this island."

"Holy crap!" Zeke said. "Not nukes."

"Where are these codes, sir?" Lea asked.

"I can't see them being stored anywhere but Blanchard's office. I'll need to go there and get them. I can give you more details later."

"Then we split up," Hawke said. "We can't waste time in case he was giving you misinformation. Can you get to his office?"

"Oh yeah," Brooke said with a crooked grin. "I've been there many times. But you take Alex with you. If the shit hits the fan, I want her on the first plane out."

"Dad!"

"It's fine," he said. "Go."

"But…"

"You'll understand when you're a mother."

"Take Reaper, Jack," Hawke said. "In case you need a small army."

The Frenchman smiled. "I'm ready."

"And Ravi," Kahlia said, pointing at the man with green eyes. "In case you run into other prisoners, and also to get you to the hangars."

"I'm ready, too," said the Brazilian.

"Looks like we got a plan," Hawke said. "Move out."

CHAPTER FIFTEEN

Making a deal with the prisoners turned out to be a smart move. First, Hawke knew most of them would be political prisoners or other people who had proved to be a major pain to the government, which in this case meant Davis Faulkner. That meant they were probably not dangerous and they were also on the same side as him and ECHO. Second, it also turned out they knew their way around the prison as if it was the back of their hands. This made reaching the hangar much easier than if they had tried to work it out for themselves.

But getting there was one thing. Fighting his way inside and securing an aircraft would be another altogether. Then there was praying Brooke, Reaper and Ravi made it to the office and back with the codes. Now, standing in the freezing night air just outside the hangar, he counted three transport aircraft – two Lockheed Hercules C-130s and a gigantic C-5 Galaxy. No contest, as far as he was concerned. He could fly the Galaxy and it was a faster, more comfortable flight with a longer range.

Up in the air, transponder off and right the hell out of here.

The problem was, it was guarded by at least a dozen men, as were the other two transport planes. This meant nearly forty armed soldiers between him and the Galaxy and they were already on high alert because of the klaxon. It wasn't all on their side, though. For one thing, they didn't have a base commander anymore, and in battle losing a leader usually meant a certain amount of delay and confusion. Second, ECHO had the element of surprise. By the looks of things, no one in the hangar knew they were right outside, not yet at least.

Then he saw something that made his day and he smiled broadly.

"What is it, Josiah?" asked a suspicious Lea. "What have you seen?"

"The Hand of God, Lea."

"Eh?"

"Over there in the corner you will see a military Humvee."

"And?"

"Look closer and you will also see a 20mm Vulcan mounted on top of it. This means party time."

"Party time, eh?"

"Yes, because in a few moments, yours truly is going to be inside that Humvee behind an electrically driven, air-cooled, six-barrel rotary cannon, firing six-thousand fifteen-hundred grain projectiles at over three thousand feet per second. At those unfortunate men over there."

"Boys and their toys," Kamala said with an eye roll.

Lea smiled. "And do you also see the three men *guarding* the Humvee, Josiah?"

"Yes, why? What's that got to do with anything?"

She shook her head. "Go and play."

He kissed her on the cheek. "I knew you'd understand. When I'm gone, brief the others. I'm going to sweep the fire to move them away from the Galaxy toward the two Hercules transporters. When they're over there, you guys split the team, get one inside the Galaxy and secure it and the other can finish off the rest of the guards. I'll use the Vulcan to take out the two Hercules planes and then they're stuck here on the island until backup arrives."

"And we'll be long gone."

He nodded unable to resist a grin. "And we'll be long gone."

"We still need Dad and the others to get here," Alex said nervously.

"They'll be fine," Kahlia said. "No one gets the better of Ravi Monteiro."

"Let's hope you're right," Alex said doubtfully. "How are you getting over to the Humvee?"

"There's a fire door just behind it," Hawke said. "Make sure you stay out of the way when the shooting starts. Jack will have more than enough time to get what he needs and get back here by the time we get the plane ready for flight."

"You've thought of everything!" Lea said with sparkling eyes. "My hero."

They kissed goodbye and Ryan rolled his eyes. "It's not exactly the time for all that."

"You're just jealous, Rupert."

"Hey! You haven't called me that for ages."

"I just feel a certain spring in my step all of a sudden," he said.

"Great, so I get called Rupert again."

Hawke shrugged. "Call it a one off."

"Have a nice day at the office, darling!" Lea called out.

*

The truth was Hawke was not having a good day at the office. He had rescued Jack Brooke and Alex Reeve from Blanchard's immediate custody and stopped their execution, but he had a long way to go to get them and the rest of the ECHO team away from Tartarus.

After the skirmish in the corridor outside their cells and the death of Blanchard and his jailers, the nest had been stirred and the hornets were flying. An emergency klaxon was sounding all over the base and powerful arc lights were flickering on all over the island. As he made his way around to the fire door at the rear entrance of the hangar, he heard the familiar sound of another Apache engine somewhere to the east.

Palm mic up to his mouth as he approached the door, gun gripped in his other hand. "Hawke to ECHO. Apache en route. Ninety degrees. Approximately a quarter of a mile out."

"Got it," Lea said.

"There could be more," Hawke said. "They could be sitting in the sky a mile away and watching everything we're doing. The first we'd know about it was when the rounds start chewing into us."

"A nice thought," Ryan said.

"Change of plan?" asked Lea.

"Yes," he said flatly. "Who wants to drive a Humvee with a cannon fixed to its roof?"

The call came back affirmative, and Hawke grinned. Thinking about whom he would prefer to take on the men surrounding the planes, he decided Nikolai had the least amount of firearms experience. He would be better suited to driving the Humvee.

"It's time to shine, Kolya. Meet me around by the rear door ASAP."

"On my way."

"Good, everyone else take cover and stand by. This could get interesting."

When Nikolai sprinted around the corner of the hangar, the Apache was almost right above them. Hawke guessed the crew were in contact with the men in the hangar because they were now splitting up into three teams. One stayed with the aircraft, the second headed out to the front, guns raised, and the third were heading over to the rear entrance.

"Heads up everyone," Hawke said into his palm mic. "The Apache's FLIR camera has picked us all up and they're giving the men in the hangar directions. They're holding back on using the rockets to minimize damage to the hangar and the planes but my guess they'll go for it if we take these soldiers out, which we're going to do any second."

"So expect the rockets, right?" Kamala said.

"No," Hawke said. "Leave that to me and Kolya."

"Things are changing fast, darling," said Scarlet.

Hawke chuckled. "And now you know why I never like to plan ahead much."

"Much?" Lea said. "Try never."

"We're going in," Hawke said. "Eyes wide open everyone."

He spun around into the doorway and opened fire on the approaching men. His aim was true and his speed was breathtaking. Pumped and ready to end the nightmare, he mercilessly ripped holes in the four soldiers jogging over to the rear door. They were dead before they hit the floor, and a shocked Nikolai made the sign of the cross over his chest.

"We can ask for forgiveness later when we're not being shot at, Kolya," he said. "Right now we need to get over to that Humvee and get things rolling."

The thoughtful Russian monk had no words, but followed the former Royal Marine Commando across the polished concrete floor to the military Humvee. When they reached it, Hawke checked the ignition and found no keys. No surprises there – on a base like this one there would be serious charges for any soldier who left keys inside a vehicle, especially a heavily armed one.

Guns sounded a few hundred yards to his left. He looked over to the hangar's main doors and saw gun muzzles flashing in the night. ECHO were engaging the other team of men. The second cohort were still standing around the planes, rifles in hand. He thought quickly. Hotwiring the Humvee would take time. Scanning the hangar, he saw an office off to his right, partially obscured by the third Hercules.

"Get inside the driver's seat and keep your head down, Kolya. I'm going to get the keys."

"But how do you know where they are?"

"Because this is a military airfield and that is the hangar's main office. Someone had to drive the Humvee over here and park it but anyone might be expected to move it. The place they would go is the main office."

"I hope you are right."

He grinned. "I'm rarely wrong."

He ran around the other side of the Humvee for some additional cover and crouch-walked across the northern part of the hangar with his head down. Keeping to the shadows, he almost made the office when one of the soldiers guarding the Hercules saw something in the corner of his eye and turned.

"Over there!" he called out to his colleagues, and then they all turned. "He's heading into the office. Open fire!"

Hawke hit the door just as the men raised their assault rifles and let rip. Crashing to the floor and rolling under the desk with his arms cradling his head, he muttered a string of curses and reached for his gun. Under a barrage of fire from half a dozen M-4 carbines, the small glass and plywood construction took seconds to tear to pieces.

Bullets drilled through the wooden walls and blasted the windows into thousands of fragments. Luckily, the desk was a heavy antique hardwood job, no doubt an original fixture of the base's early days, and he was able to upturn it and use it for cover. He saw a hook key cabinet on the wall to his side, about as old as the desk and reached out and knocked it off the wall. Hooked to one nail, it tumbled down onto the floor and crashed beside him.

The act triggered another savage fusillade from outside the office but he had the Humvee's ignition key. Then he peered over the top through the smoky, dusty room and prepared to take aim and return fire when he saw something that made his blood run cold.

One of the soldiers was now holding an M320 grenade launcher module and pointing it right in his face.

"Fire!"

It was a corporal's voice. Hawke saw his insignia. Then, a bright flash and the grenade was airborne.

CHAPTER SIXTEEN

Hawke's options were not good. Of all the available choices, he quickly dismissed the idea of taking a grenade hit direct to his face. He also knew the upturned desk didn't have what it took to shield from a 40mm grenade exploding in a confined area like what was currently left of the office. Outside the office in the hangar, the rest of the soldiers were still holding their assault rifles in case he decided to make a break for it.

These thoughts flashed through his mind in half a second. They had to, the grenade launcher's muzzlc velocity was seventy-six meters per second and the man holding it was only twice that distance from the office. That gave him the other one and a half seconds to spring up from his position behind the upturned oak table and throw himself through the blasted window to his left.

His upper body made it but his legs were still inside when the grenade ripped into the wrecked office and fiercely exploded. As he had expected, the shockwave helped him on his way, but came with an unwanted fireball, wrapping around his lower body. He felt a searing heat envelop him as he crashed to the floor beneath the fireball which shot out above him another twenty meters in all directions.

The armed soldiers swivelled and aimed at him, but his plan was good. The accompanying smoke from the blast now obscured him as he rolled over the broken wood and shattered glass splinters. The men fired blindly, raking the smoke cloud with bullets but he had already rolled to his feet and dived behind the Humvee.

"All good, Kolya?" he said as he tossed him the key.

"Not really, but I'm glad you are alive."

"Which is more than can be said about the rest of these guys. Start her up mate and drive forward into the smoke."

"I was going to ask if you are insane, but this I already know."

"I prefer *special*, but whatever. Now get going."

As Nikolai turned on the engine and pulled the Humvee slowly through the smoke toward the soldiers, Hawke clambered into the back and up through the top hatch where the Vulcan was mounted on the roof. Bearing the moniker *Hand of God*, and with good reason, the M61 20mm Vulcan was a serious, heavy piece of kit. Originally fitted to the wing pylons of USAF F-16 and F-18 fighter jets, the gun's terrifying cycle rate was designed to destroy the target in a few seconds so a speeding jet could maintain its aim and get the job done fast before turning.

Luckily, the weapon was already fully loaded, as Hawke had hoped it might be, because it was a tough weapon to feed ammo into. Now, as the Vulcan drove through the smoke filling the hangar, he activated the gun and swivelled it across to the soldiers, opening fire on them with one of the meanest guns on the planet.

The massive rounds ripped them to the pieces and chewed into the concrete floor, blasting fist-sized chunks up into the air around their dead bodies. Concrete dust and powder mixed with the smoke and dust as Hawke coughed in the choking atmosphere and swivelled the Vulcan around. Then, he pointed the six-barrel rotary nightmare at the other team of soldiers standing around the second Hercules.

They were already making tracks inside the transport plane, but they would find no sanctuary there, not from

Hawke and his Vulcan. From the other side of the hangar, he opened fire not on the men but on the wings of the Hercules, drilling the enormous rounds into the fuel tanks and igniting the kerosene inside.

"Turn, Kolya! Go back!"

Kolya spun the wheel hard to the left and turned, rumbling the big fat tires over some of the dead soldiers as the Hercules detonated. Hawke ducked down through the hatch and shut his eyes, feeling the immense shockwave and heat blast race over the top of the Humvee and violently shake it on its suspension. The inside of the heavy vehicle rattled like a drum in the blast. The noise was like being inside an exploding volcano and then the inside of the hangar was in total darkness. Smoke from the burning plane and spilled fuel and oil billowed up into the air and cut out all light. Men screamed. More alarms shrieked from speakers on the walls.

Hawke reached into his pack and pulled his night vision goggles. "Do the same, Kolya."

"Already on it, Joe."

With the visor fitted neatly over his head, he moved back up through the hatch and resumed his position behind the Vulcan. In the smoke-filled horror of the hangar, he avoided looking at the burning wreck of the aircraft – it was too bright through the goggles – but noticed the remaining soldiers sprinting for safety outside. He considered cutting them down, but then he saw them fall dead to the floor anyway. ECHO had taken them out from their position at the front of the hangar.

That left the other Hercules and the Apache. Swivelling the six big ugly barrels around, he raised his palm mic to his mouth and ordered Kolya to drive over to the remaining Hercules. The Russian responded instantly, steering to the right and cruising through the burning debris strewn all over the hangar's floor. The handful of soldiers remaining on guard were taking up a defensive position behind the aircraft, having seen what happened to their colleagues. They sighted the Humvee and opened fire.

This meant nothing to Hawke. Ordering Kolya to keep down behind the dash and increase speed, he unleashed total hell on the surviving guards. The massive twenty mil rounds ripped through the Hercules's forward bogie, blasting holes through the oleo cylinder and scattering pieces of the chewed-up trunnion braces all over the concrete.

He fired again, releasing dozens more of the chunky rounds. The Vulcan's terrifying muzzle velocity ensured the total annihilation of the rest of the forward bogie and now it snapped in two, collapsing to the hangar floor. The entire front end of the massive Hercules transporter now toppled forward and smashed to the ground in an enormous ground-shaking crash. Metal bent, windows blew out and the props back on the main wings crumpled into the concrete as if they were made of aluminum foil.

This gave Hawke two advantages. First, the men taking cover behind it no longer had the clear shot they needed to take out the Humvee. Second, he had the cover he needed for Kolya to drive around to the front of the crippled aircraft and get to their position. He knew the Humvee could drive faster than they could run, after all.

"Get to the other side, Kolya."

"On it."

As the Russian monk raced the Hummer across the hangar and passed in front of the Hercules, Hawke now swung the Vulcan around to his right and saw what he'd expected to see – the soldiers were fleeing to the rear of the aircraft. They were trying to reach the section under the wings where the main bogies were just about holding up and allowing enough elevation below the plane for them to cut through to the other side.

One of the fleeing soldiers turned on his heel and swung his rifle around, ripping a few holes in the front of the Humvee and blasting its main lights out. Hawke aimed the cannon at him and let rip, shredding him into chunks and blasting him all over the floor. The other men were still sprinting away, but they were still under orders to kill him. When out of sight, they would regroup and come back at him, and he couldn't let that happen. If they killed him, Kolya and then the others would be next. He felt a twinge of guilt but shook it off fast.

Opening fire with the rotary cannon, he swept the muzzle from side to side. The beast of a weapon unleashed yet more hell onto Faulkner's forces. The ammo belt clattered as it hungrily ate up the rounds and spat them at the men. The cannon's wild *chank chank chank* filled the air like a growling animal. Cases flew out of the ejector port, smoke was everywhere and the mechanical whine of the rotor assembly cried out above it all.

Then the men were gone, cut into chunks by the devastating gun.

"We did it!" Kolya said.

Hawke quit firing, already repressing the memory of the soldiers' deaths from his mind. "Not yet. Get her outside, Kolya. We need to take out the Apache. The rest of the team are still in trouble."

CHAPTER SEVENTEEN

And Lea Donovan *was* in trouble. Pinned down on her own behind a garage block full of Jeeps, she had gotten separated from the rest of the team in a skirmish when the first Hercules went up and exploded in the hangar. For a second, she thought Hawke and Nikolai must be dead. The blast was just too great for anyone to have survived. The fireball was colossal and the thick, black smoke noxious and choking.

Then she had heard their voices over the comms and breathed a sigh of relief. But not for long, because now the Apache was swivelling around in the air and heading straight for her. The attack chopper had been hovering above the hangar but ascended a few hundred feet and backed off after the explosion. That was when she decided to make a break for it and get to the hangar to help Hawke.

She ignored the others' calls to stay in the cover of one of the smaller helicopter hangars and instead sprinted across the apron, but the Apache had tracked her on its FLIR camera and opened fire. The rounds from its chin-mounted chain-gun nipped at her heels and chased her all the way across the asphalt. She knew she was never going to make the hangar and swerved off to her right and dived into the garage block with only seconds to spare.

Now the chopper was angling around and descending, aiming its formidable arsenal right at her and preparing to open fire. She guessed the only reason she wasn't already dead was because the crew were waiting for permission from the base's second-in-command to blow up the garage block and take out the half-dozen Jeeps parked inside. When that permission came through, they would blast her into a million pieces, never to be found or seen again.

She was trapped and running out of options fast. Running for the hangar was insane – they would cut her to ribbons before she got ten yards from the entrance. She considered going out in a blaze of glory and burning across the apron in one of the Jeeps. The end result would be the same, only with burning gasoline and pieces of torn metal and plastic all over the place.

Her mind raced.

You don't outrun an Apache attack helicopter in a Jeep, Lea Kaitlin Donovan. Think!

But what to do?

Then the chopper descended again, now almost level with the garage. Its angular black front, chain-gun and wing pylons loaded with missiles and rockets made her blood run cold. She heard firing. It was ECHO, from across the apron inside one of the chopper hangars. They were shooting at the Apache and trying to distract it to give her some to get away, but their cover fire wasn't working this time. They were too far away and their firepower just wasn't enough.

Then, she saw dozens of prisoners running into view. They were trying to draw the gunship's fire. She couldn't believe it when the chopper turned and fired on them. They ran in all directions but the Apache effortlessly mowed them down with a combination of the chain-gun and Hellfire missiles. She slid down behind the Jeep, unable to process the senseless carnage she had just witnessed.

Maybe this time she had simply run shit out of luck.

Then, Hawke.

She watched through the garage door as the Humvee burst out of the smoky hangar like a bullet from a gun. Dragging a vortex of smoke in its wake, it swerved hard to the left and headed straight for the Apache, weaving around the prisoner's dead bodies. She had never been so glad to see anyone in her entire life. Kolya steered the speeding vehicle in an aggressive clockwise arc as Hawke stood up through the roof hatch and swung the six-barrel beast up into the aim and opened fire on the Apache.

The pilot had clocked the threat and already taken evasive manoeuvres. She knew Hawke would know its strategy. He had flown attack helicopters many times. Sure enough, it gained elevation in the snow-scratched sky and turned on the new threat. The crew inside were busy working together like a well-oiled machine to neutralize the threat and then clean up the stragglers on the ground below. It opened fire with its chain-gun and sent Kolya swerving to the left in a blaze of squealing tires and burning rubber. She watched Hawke rotate the weapon, fearless in the face of the rounds ripping past him on both sides.

He fired back with the Vulcan and the Apache banked hard to the left and pulled back again. Hawke's rounds traced past the aircraft and ripped out into the dark, frozen night above the ocean. He fired again, and again the chopper banked away and then returned fire, this time with another of the Hellfire missiles.

Face numbed by the freezing temperatures, Lea watched on with horror. Across the apron in the helicopter hangar, the rest of the ECHO team did the same, hearts in mouths. Kolya accelerated and spun the wheel hard to the left. Seconds from impact, the missile flashed past them and made contact with the hangar's far west side, blowing the end wall and part of the roof into sections of burning sheet metal in an enormous fireball.

Hawke was already pivoting around and taking another aim at the Apache. He opened fire as Kolya righted the Humvee and performed another wide arc. Now the two vehicles were racing toward each other across the apron. The Apache let another missile rip and once again it streaked across the sky directly toward the Humvee.

Kolya steered away and Hawke swivelled the gun and opened fire again. The chaos was almost impossible to take in and Lea felt like closing her eyes. Then, she saw the Vulcan's rounds finally make contact with the Apache and chew into it, hard. They blew the chain-gun to pieces and blasted fist-sized holes in the aircraft's nose. Windows shattered and exploded as more rounds tore the rotors to shreds. The crew struggled to keep their machine airborne, but Hawke was relentless.

He fired again and again at the stricken aircraft, straight into the cockpit and ripped the entire crew to pieces, tracking them through the air with the Vulcan as the helicopter plummeted through the air. It hit the ground and exploded in a massive fireball, sending jets of burning fuel flying off into the air above the apron like something on the Fourth of July or Bonfire Night. Only this was no celebration. This was the deaths of an Apache crew.

But they were trying to kill them, Lea told herself. We've done this before. They were following the orders of Davis Faulkner. We did the right thing. Her thoughts were interrupted by the sound of Jack Brooke's voice on the comms. He had found the deactivation codes and was on his way back over to the hangar. Thank God, she thought with a silent prayer.

Kolya turned and pulled up outside the helicopter hangar and she watched the ECHO team clambering up all over the Humvee. Some went inside it, others clung to the side. She recognized the woman with the tattoos but there was someone else there, a man with salt and pepper hair shaved down short and a thin, leathery face. He was hanging onto the side of the Humvee just in front of Kamala.

The Russian monk cruised it across the apron, steering gently to drive around the burning, smoking wreckage of the Apache. As she wandered out of the garage and straightened her jacket, they pulled up in a smooth arc in front of her.

Hawke spun the cannon away and took off his night vision goggles. “Fancy a ride?”

“Maybe after a shower,” she said, crisply, gazing at the strange man.

“Oh, meet Tawan,” Scarlet said. “He’s one of the felons here.”

“He’s a relic smuggler from Bangkok,” Kahlia said. “And a serious fighter. You could use him.”

“Hey,” Lea said to him.

He nodded but said nothing.

Hawke laughed. “Hop on board. Jack, Reaper, Ravi and Alex are waiting in what’s left of the hangar for us to get that Galaxy fired up and fly out of here. We have a presidency to save and after tonight, something tells me Faulkner’s not going down without the fight of his life.”

CHAPTER EIGHTEEN

President Davis Faulkner regarded the report in his hands with a mix of fear and disbelief. His Chief-of-Staff Josh Muston had just received the intelligence from a senior CIA official and trusted friend, so it was doubtful any mistake had been made. However fantastic and unbelievable it sounded, he had to believe it, and yet in his heart he hoped it was wrong.

"And your man is totally sure this has happened?" he asked.

"Yes sir, Mr President. We can trust anything from this source. Less than thirty minutes ago, the ECHO team executed a raid on Tartarus, killed dozens of military personnel serving on the base, including the base commander, and extricated and freed Jack Brooke and Alex Reeve."

The fear subsided and a new emotion emerged – an emotion of raw rage, wild like a caged beast poked one time too many.

"How the hell could this happen, Josh? You told me Tartarus was the last word in total security, a place we could keep problems out of the light forever. A place we could hide assets in total safety. Now I find out a team of ragbag misfit terrorist sons-of-bitches has just walked in and helped themselves to whatever they fuck they want there."

Josh's eyes widened at the bad language. Faulkner was an angry and power-hungry individual, but he could usually be relied upon for his cold and cynical calculation.

Outbursts of cursing were rare and always meant he was on the verge of a full meltdown.

"They're not going to get away with it, sir," he said, trying to sooth the incipient rage across the other side of the Resolute Desk. "We already have jets from the Roosevelt searching for the stolen Galaxy."

Faulkner narrowed his eyes. "Galaxy?"

Muston took a short step back and tried to look nonchalant. Like everything was under full control. "They took a C-5 Galaxy military transport from the main hangar."

Faulkner smashed his fist down on the desk. "Damn it! This is totally unacceptable! You mean to say, we let those bastards get onto our most secure military location, break a former President of the United States out of a maximum security solitary confinement cell and steal one of our god-*damn* transporter jets?"

"I know, it sounds bad…"

"Bad? Is that all you have to say? You clearly have no idea how close you are to getting fired right now."

"We can handle this, Mr President."

"Wanna start explaining how?"

"Yes, sir. Like I just said, we're already in pursuit of them."

"Go on."

"The USS Roosevelt Strike Group is in the Bering Sea on high-end exercises right now and when they received a radio transmission from the island saying it was under attack, Captain Donohue sent a couple of Hornets up to check out what's going on."

Faulkner shifted in his seat and reached for a cigar. "And what was '*going on*' on the island? Anyone know any concrete details about this raid yet?"

"The island is mostly untouched, but the airfield aprons were totally smashed. The main hangar has been destroyed completely and the Hornet pilots reported the burning wrecks of two Hercules transport aircraft and an Apache."

"ECHO did all that?"

"Yes, sir. Security cameras on the base picked them up a few times when they got inside the prison. They took the cameras out fast enough but we got some shots. Hawke, Donovan, Reno and Sloane. They were all there."

Faulkner felt his rage subside again and the fear began to crawl back up inside him like a thousand spiders. "They're coming for me, Josh. I know it in here." He tapped his chest with his hand, cigar held loosely in his fingers. Loose ash fell on the desk and smoke from the tip twirled up into the air between them. "They're coming for me."

"They're not going to get that far, sir."

"You'd better hope not. For one thing, if I'm going down, you're coming with me. Whether that's arrest and trials or taking a bullet."

Muston paled. "It won't come to that, Mr President."

Faulkner was interrupted by a hurried knock at the door. "Get that."

"Sir." Muston paced across the large rug in the center of the Oval Office and swung open the door to reveal a young man in a USAF uniform. He was holding a plastic folder in his right hand.

"We have the recon you ordered, Mr Muston."

"Great. Thanks, Major."

"Sir."

Muston walked it back across the room and stood back in front of the desk.

"We have no boots on the island yet, so we don't know what the interiors of the buildings look like, but we do already have some reconnaissance images, sir."

Faulkner's eyes narrowed further. "Recon?"

"You were in a meeting with Ambassador Zhukov, sir, so I took the liberty of re-tasking one of the reconnaissance satellites." He gingerly placed the folder on the desk in front of the red-faced president.

Faulkner took a long suck on the fat cigar and opened the plastic folder. His eyes widened as he took in the short series of satellite reconnaissance photos of Tartarus. Smoke poured from the main hangar. Two burned-out shells that used to be transporter planes. Blast craters in the airfield's apron that looked like it had been delivered by some major league ordinance. Chaos everywhere. Dead men were sprawled out like broken dolls all over the place. In the last few images, a C-5 Galaxy was lifting off the runway and leaving the island to the east.

"This has the signature of a well-planned attack," Muston said.

"This concerns me greatly, Josh."

"The Hornet pilots are working with the satellite data to close in on them, sir. When they find them, all you have to do is give the word and they're all blown out of the sky. If anything, it might be better this way."

Faulkner felt a glimmer of hope. "Damn it, you could be right. This way there will be no bodies and no evidence. They'll go down in international waters. We'll still have to think of something to explain it, of course. Brooke, especially."

"Of course, sir. Leave that to me. We're already thinking along the lines of producing some sort of deep fake video message from Brooke."

"After this mess, is that wise?"

"Sir?"

"No, I don't like it. Someone will figure it out. Go old school."

"Yes, sir. But don't worry. It's containable."

"It had better be, Josh. If they get to me, if they get *here*," he wafted the cigar around to indicate the Oval Office, "then we're all finished. Not least of all because if they get here, they'll get their hands on the Citadel files. The Land of the Gods, Josh. They can never know what we know."

Muston started to look nervous. "That won't happen, Mr President."

"Let's hope not. What we found in the Citadel is classified at the highest level available to this country's security services. Never, and I mean *never* can that information get into the wrong hands." A big suck on the cigar and a long exhalation into the room. The fragrant smoke drifted up to the ceiling. "ECHO are the wrong hands, Josh. They'll learn things no ordinary man or woman could ever understand. The secrets of the white robed guards and those *weapons*… They might even get some damned stupid idea in their heads about *doing the right thing* and transparency and all that crap and take it public."

"That can never happen, sir."

"Damn right it can never happen!" he snapped.

Muston tried to sooth him again. "There's no way ECHO or Brooke can get anywhere near the United States, let alone the Oval Office and the Citadel files."

Faulkner was silent a long time. When he spoke, his voice was much calmer and cold. "And if they do, there's always Perses and Krios."

Muston's face grew even paler. "I hope it won't come to that. Not Krios, anyway."

"You're not losing your nerve on me, are you Josh?"

"No, sir."

"Good. Krios is a whole different ballgame, even I'll admit that, but Operation Perses was initiated for good reason, Josh and I will order its use if I have to. Any sign

ECHO comes anywhere near the US, I will order the activation of the Perses nuclear weapons and take out those three cities. The total devastation caused will bring this country to its knees and the hunger for a great and powerful leader will be almost insatiable."

"Yes, sir. Indeed it will."

"Indeed it will, Mr Muston, and I'm just the man for the job. If those bombs go off, not only will ECHO be fully implicated as the terror group who planted them, but my power as a leader will grow beyond all measure. I'm already working on scrapping the Twenty-Second Amendment."

Muston's eyes flicked up from the satellite pictures to the man behind the desk. He was grinning widely now, like that cat that got the cream. "You want to end the two-term limit for sitting presidents?"

"It's holding me back, Josh. How can I do the work I need to do in such a short time limit? Thanks to my having to step in midway through Brooke's first term, I'm practically a one-term president."

"That's presuming you win the next election, sir."

Faulkner glanced at his subordinate, eyes narrowing again. He twirled his cigar, now burnt halfway down. "Why, whose side are you on, Josh? Of course I'm going to win the next election. Perses would certainly see to that. The American people usually vote for the status quo in times of great crisis. They are a smart citizenry. They like order. Stability. Continuity."

"Yes they do, sir, and you're the man to deliver it."

Faulkner took another long drag on the cigar and let the thick smoke roll around his mouth for a few seconds before exhaling. "You know, the more I think about it, the more I start to think this escape plan being conducted by ECHO could be the best thing that ever happened to me.

I want you to call the captain of the Roosevelt and tell him to turn those jets around."

"Sir?"

"I want ECHO to land in the United States. I want CCTV and photos of them landing and walking and breathing right here in the US. A failed coup led by an embittered and deranged Jack Brooke. Then we activate Perses and show the world once and for all exactly what sort of terrorist scum Brooke and ECHO really are."

Muston looked at him with uncertainty, then pulled himself up straight. "Yes sir, Mr President. I'll contact the Strike Group immediately. You want me to continue the satellite tracking operation?"

"Yes. We need to know where they're going to land so we can get the photographic evidence. We need to stay one step ahead of them. This time, it really is the end of ECHO and Brooke, and then we can work on my polices for my second and third terms. And maybe even my fourth and fifth. Let's kick FDR right out of the history books, right?"

Muston gave a nervous laugh and left the room.

Faulkner closed his eyes and began dreaming of the New World Order he could start building just as soon as Hawke and the others were executed for the most terrible terror attacks ever perpetrated on US soil.

Suddenly, the world seemed full of hope all over again.

CHAPTER NINETEEN

Hawke looked at Jack Brooke with disbelief. "Blanchard actually told you that?"

Brooke nodded his head. "It's hard to believe, isn't it?"

"So, Faulkner set up some kind of nuclear apocalyptic dead man's switch to stop us getting to him in DC." As the Englishman repeated what Brooke had just told him, his words were soft in the gentle hum of the Galaxy's cockpit. Ahead, a faint pink glow on the eastern horizon was slowly erasing the stars above them.

He glanced at the instrument panel and took note of their present position and speed. At this rate they would be approaching the north-western coast of California in less than a couple of hours, arriving just before lunch local time. Everyone on board presumed they were being tracked by satellite after the lethal assault on Tartarus, but no one could explain why there had been no fighter jets sent out to attack them.

Something was up, and after a discussion with Jack Brooke, they were starting to get more dots to put together.

"What else did he tell you?" Lea asked.

"Really not all that much else," said Brooke with an affable shrug. "I wish there were more, but it wasn't exactly a friendly chitchat between old buddies. He was about to order my execution and guessed he could get away with telling me what is clearly highly restricted information. All I know is, Faulkner has created a sort of ring of steel around his presidency in the form of three nuclear bombs which were stored, off the record, on Tartarus."

"A ring of steel?"

Brooke nodded. "Those were almost Blanchard's exact words. He described it as a dead man's switch and said if we tried to get anywhere near Faulkner he'd bring the Apocalypse to the United States. He said it was a scorched hearth policy and I don't think he was confused or lying about it. I think he was a smart man who was telling me the truth. I also think he was kind of scared of Davis Faulkner. I could see it in his eyes when he was telling me."

"Scared of Faulkner, or scared of what he might do," Lea said.

"That's about the size of it," Brooke said. "A man like Faulkner trades on his unpredictable nature. People don't like that. They want to know what to expect next. With a man like Faulkner you don't get that. He changes his mind at the drop of a hat. Switches strategy without warning. Whatever Blanchard told us might have already changed. We have to plan for everything."

"We can do this," Hawke said.

"We only have nine people who can fight," Nikolai said, glancing at Alex. "Twelve if you count our new friends from the prison."

"Wrong," Hawke said, turning to see Kahlia, Ravi and Tawan sitting in the cabin behind the expansive cockpit. "We'll have lucky thirteen, and let me explain why. Alex is joining us."

From the back of the cockpit, she looked at him like he was crazy. Pointing to her wheelchair, she said, "Aren't you forgetting something?"

"Yeah, about that," Hawke said, reaching into his pack. "Recently, when we were in the Land of the Gods, I took a good few pints of local spring water from the

Citadel, in my canteen." He pulled out the scratched, dented canteen and held it up in front of him. "And this is it."

Alex's eyes widened like saucers, but were soon darkened by doubts and fears. "It can't be!"

"We think it is," Hawke said. "We don't know much about the White Robed Guardians we encountered in the Citadel yet – I'm hoping Faulkner's Oval Office files will shed some light on that situation – but we know they fought like demons to protect the place. I think this is the elixir we encountered before, only in much larger quantities. I'm hoping it gets you out of that chair, and not only that. Because there is so much more of it, I'm also hoping we can analyze it better and figure out how it works."

Lea said, "And maybe even produce enough of it ourselves to ensure you, and anyone else who needs it in the world, can have it whenever it's needed."

Brooke watched as Hawke opened the lid and held the canteen up to Alex. Behind her shoulder, back in the cabin, the others peered through into the cockpit to get a better view. "Here, take some."

She hesitated and then took the canteen. "You're sure it's okay?"

"No, not at all," he said. "But we've all had a sip and we're still here."

"You're not going to make a joke and fall to the floor, clutching your throat or something?"

"Not this time," he said. "Sorry, but this is too serious."

Alex tipped the canteen up and let the magical water flow inside her mouth. Released from the metal container, the elixir sparkled on her lips in little gold flashes. "Oh, wow. That's weird."

"What's weird about it?" Brooke asked. He was sitting in the first officer's seat and now he was twisted fully around and staring with concern at his daughter.

"Just... weird. I remember now, from before."

"It's the water of life," Lea said.

Alex handed the container back to Hawke. "Thanks, now we wait, I guess."

"And talk," Lea said. "Did Blanchard say where these nukes were situated?"

"He did not," Brooke said. "But when Reaper and Miss Keahi and I raided Blanchard's office to retrieve the deactivation codes, we found all the information on Operation Perses that we need. There's one in San Francisco, one in Chicago and one in New York City."

"Bloody hell!" Ryan said.

"He's not screwing around," Scarlet said. "Those are some of the biggest populations in the entire country."

"And they're all big places," Lea said. "Do we know where the bombs are located within in each city?"

Brooke nodded. "We do. Each one was placed as close to the geographic center of each metropolis to ensure maximum destruction and fallout. The San Francisco bomb is inside the Museum of Modern Art on Third Street, just south of downtown. The Chicago one was hidden in the Navy Pier, also to ensure the entire downtown district is wiped from the map. In New York City, they put the bomb inside the Stock Exchange. The exact locations are all marked here, so everyone take a look. Their goal isn't just to destroy the city and kill millions of New Yorkers, but also to trigger a financial meltdown across the entire country, maybe the entire world."

"Holy crap," Zeke said. "This is worse than I thought."

"It's worse than we all thought," Hawke said. "Luckily, we know about it and we're on the case. The first thing we need to do is break into three teams. One goes to each nuke location, armed with the correct deactivation code. Next, we need to make sure we all act at the same time. If Faulkner gets word that we've taken out one of the nukes while the other two are still operational, he could do the unthinkable and detonate the remaining bombs."

"Not a best case scenario," Lea said quietly.

"No, not a good place to be," said Brooke. "We can't let that happen. Under any circumstances."

"All right." Hawke clapped his hands together. "Let's lift the mood with some good old-fashioned tactical discussions!"

Scarlet laughed. "Careful Joe, or you might turn into Ryan."

"Hey!" the young man said. "Will these cutting barbs never end?"

"Unlikely," she said with a wink. "I get too much out of them."

"And moving on," Hawke said, smiling at his team. "Let's get to business. We have enough time to plan this out and get some shuteye before we land. We can do this."

"I sure pray you're right," Zeke said. "Because if we're all just high on hopium, then we're walking into a nuclear apocalypse and the end of ECHO and probably the United States."

"Great pep talk, Ezekiel," Scarlet said. "Do you do corporate events as well?"

He laughed. "I go with the money, babe."

"There's not going to be any apocalypse," Lea said. "And we're not high on *hopium* either. We know what we're doing and we've done similar missions before. We can and will do this."

"Lea's right," Hawke said, his face an eerie amber in the glow of the flight deck instruments. "There's just too much riding on this one even to contemplate failure."

"And Ryan and I have a little idea, too," Alex said.

"What sort of idea?" Hawke asked.

"We'll keep it to ourselves for now, but we think some computer research might help the team right now, especially Dad."

"Mysterious," Lea said.

Alex smiled. "We'll see. We need some time."

"You have the rest of the flight," Hawke said with a smile. He checked his watch. "Time's moving on. We'd better get to business..."

*

Sir Richard Eden stared at the man in disbelief. Tall, slim and tanned, Jonathan Atha was a former MI5 intelligence officer and old friend of his going way back. They had worked hard on dozens of cases together all over the world and played even harder in cities from Marrakesh to Mumbai and Tallinn to Tokyo. Now, his old friend was a pixelated distortion of the real thing on a dimly lit Zoom call, hastily arranged behind his jailers' backs.

"It's good to see you, old boy," Eden said.

"You too," Atha said. "What's all this about house arrest?"

"All true, I'm afraid. I've been locked away at my place in Oxfordshire for some time now but there's hope. More than that I can't say right now. It's not a trust thing, Jonathan. More to do with walls having ears, or in this case, cyber-eavesdropping."

"Unlikely, but I understand."

"What did you want to talk to me about? I haven't got long. They do random checks on me and I haven't seen anyone for over an hour."

"Then I'll get straight to the point. You remember Nigel?"

"If you're about Lieutenant Gambles, then of course. One of my best officers, both in the regiment and during my time at MI5."

"I am indeed talking about Lieutenant Gambles."

"Not come to any harm, I hope."

"Not at all. But it's not good news. He made contact with me a few hours ago with something important he thought I ought to know."

"Go on."

"He overheard some chatter recently about Joseph Kashala."

Eden's heart sank. "King Kashala?"

"The very same."

"Not good."

"No. We all heard about your team's thrashing of the old Congolese warlord, but it seems he didn't stay down very long. There's word he's back on the scene. Nigel looked into the chatter and it looks like Kashala has rebuilt his notorious Blood Crew and is going back into business."

"Business?"

"Unspecified, but probably his extensive smuggling operations. That includes drugs, arms and people. There's also word he's planning a major terror attack somewhere. No more details, I'm afraid. They're working on it and when I know more, you'll know more. That's presuming I can get in contact with you, naturally."

"Thanks, Jonathan. I appreciate it, but if ECHO fail in their current mission it's doubtful any of them, or I, will be around to take on Kashala."

"Sounds ominous."

"I wish I could say more, but things are pretty bad right now."

"Then you're not going to like what I have to say next."

Eden's heart sank lower. "All right. No sugar-coating, please."

"Nigel says he's also overheard chatter referring to a much bigger enemy from your past, someone we all thought was long gone. Apparently, he's also back in business and with a very interesting partner, whose name I think you might also recognize."

"Who?"

"None other than…"

The image flicked off. Eden scanned the tiny screen of his smartphone and saw the internet signal had been cut. Faulkner's goons here at the house must have worked out he was in communication with someone else on the outside. He cursed, got to his feet and began pacing the room. Who was Jonathan talking about? What had Nigel discovered? Who was the big enemy from his past? What was this mysterious partnership? The questions tumbled in his mind like an avalanche. He heard boots on the stairs outside his room. No time to think, he jumped on the desk, pulled back the section of ceiling coving and hid the phone inside a small hole there. Then he replaced the coving and walked back over to the desk.

Calm, measured. Hands folded behind head and eyes closed. Not in any way making illicit communications with the outside world.

The door burst open and two men stormed into the room. One had drawn a handgun. The other unarmed man approached first. "Where is it?"

Eden opened one eye. "I'm sorry?"

"The phone. Where is it?"

"I have no idea what you're…"

His inquisitor turned to the man with the gun. Get Richardson, then I want both of you to turn this room upside down until you find it."

"Yes, sir."

Eden closed his eye and sighed. Looked like it was going to be a long night.

And he suddenly had a lot to think about.

CHAPTER TWENTY

Hawke leaned forward over the yoke and stared out at the sky. The day had dawned, but they were short at this time of year. He made a quick calculation and figured out it would be dark by the time the other teams reached Chicago and New York, but the San Francisco team would be working in the late afternoon. Not a massive problem, but a night raid would have been easier.

Checking the instruments one more time, he now turned to Brooke who was still sitting beside him in the first officer's seat. Behind them, Lea dozed in the navigator's seat. Behind her, Alex and Ryan were asleep in the jump seats after a long few hours working away on their laptops.

"All right, time to descend," Hawke said, winding the small altitude control down to five thousand feet. "When we get under ten thousand I'll open up the back and you can throw the Humvees into the drink."

Brooke frowned. "Huh?"

"What the hell are you talking about, Joe?" Ryan said with a yawn.

"Weight, Rupert."

"You said that was a one-off." He sounded more awake now, and was sitting up in his seat and rubbing his eyes. "The Rupert thing…you said it was a one-off."

"Yeah, sorry. Make it a two-off."

"What about weight?" Lea said, also fully awake now.

"We can't just fly in and land at San Francisco International," he said. "I know Alex and Ryan cut the satellite link feeding them our location, plus our course change into the international jet routes and waypoints following that would have made it hard for them to find us, but…"

"But it's doesn't take Sherlock Holmes to guess we're going to come in at SF International," Brooke said. "Especially if they think we already know the locations of the bombs. They'll be waiting there with open arms."

"And a lot of guns," Ryan said.

Lea sighed. "And a warrant for our arrests."

"Exactly," Hawke said. "Which brings me to weight. I used the flight management system here to locate another airport fairly close to San Francisco. It's called Half Moon Bay and it's right out on the coast. It's around thirty miles south of the city, so if we can borrow some smaller aircraft from the airport there – maybe a couple of smaller jets and a helicopter, we can split into three teams and get to the locations of the various bombs."

"Borrow?" Lea said with a smile.

He shrugged. "Yeah… sort of."

"So back to weight?" Ryan asked.

"Runway length," Brooke said. "Am I right?"

"Indeed you are," said Hawke, watching as the altitude ticked down toward five thousand feet. Ahead of them, the coast of California was starting to come into view but offered a gloomy, foggy vista. "According to the FMS, the runway is four-thousand nine-hundred feet long, which is a slight problem as we'll probably need a bit longer than that to land in this thing."

"Unless we make ourselves lighter," Ryan said.

"Much lighter," said Hawke. "If we can get everything out, we stand a better chance of not crashing off the runway, and in this case that means some fields and houses and then the ocean."

"Now I can see the logic," Ryan said. "So we need to get everything out?"

"All non-essential items – the Humvees, all the cargo… *you.*"

Ryan gave a sarcastic laugh. "And here I was, thinking you'd lost your sense of humor."

"How could I lose my sense of humor," Hawke replied. "You're one of my best friends."

Ryan got up and punched him on the shoulder. "You old kidder."

"Less of the old, and get to work."

*

Ryan Bale watched the cargo ramp open up at the back of the Galaxy. The aircraft had once broken the world record for the heaviest airdrop when the USAF dropped seventy-three paratroopers from the 82nd Airborne and four Sheridan tanks weighing more than eighty-five tons. Tonight was slightly more modest, involving two Humvees and some steal crates full of supplies for Tartarus, mostly food and drink.

When the ramp was fully open, he looked out across the tops of the clouds and was struck by the thought of just how far he had come in just a few short years with ECHO. From a no-hoper dropout hacker to this – rolling Humvees out of the back of a stolen C-5 Galaxy on his way to restore the rightful President of the United States of America. It just didn't seem real. In his heart, he harbored fears that one day it might all come to an end, even if they succeeded tonight.

Maybe Eden would say he'd had enough. Maybe Joe and Lea would decide to pack it all in to start a family somewhere quiet. It wasn't very hard to imagine them in a cottage somewhere on the Irish coast raising their kids. Others were even less likely to hang around. Lexi? A loose cannon who could disappear at any moment. The call of Monique and the twins might become too powerful for Reaper. Scarlet had talked in quiet moments of spending more time with her brother Sir Spencer Sloane and the small unit he had put together to track down the infamous Nazi Gold Train.

And where would that leave him? It seemed everyone had another life waiting for them except him. With Maria dead, he had nothing outside of ECHO. It was his career and his family and his entire life. Maybe he had become a little too dependent on it all. The wind whipped inside the back of the plane and rippled his shirt and hair. Cold, but not too bad now they were down below pressurization altitude.

"Snap out of it, fucknuts."

Startled, he turned and saw Scarlet Sloane. She was standing behind him, tethered to the plane's hull just like he was. Nothing like two seconds with Cairo to get you right back into reality again. "Ah, I was just thinking about you, *not*."

"I don't give a damn what you were thinking about, boy. It's time to roll these Hummers out of that door. We're landing in twenty."

"But won't that make the USAF rather cross?" he asked with sly grin.

"I think we crossed that line when we blew up Tartarus, rescued the president and stole this aircraft. I say we go for the whole hog, don't you?"

"Indeed I do."

Behind them, Reaper was unstrapping the first Humvee. He paused as the plane buffeted in some turbulence, then reached inside and released the parking brake. Moving around to the front, he pushed hard and began to roll it toward the rear cargo door. Slow at first, it soon gathered pace. Ryan and Scarlet stepped back against the hull as the Frenchman rolled it past them and then down the ramp and out of the door.

Reaper didn't even look at it. As he turned and padded back to the remaining Humvee, Ryan and Scarlet watched it tumble surreally through the air behind the plane. It ate up the five thousand feet in seconds and then crashed into the Pacific in a giant splash. With the white water still bubbling on the surface far below, Reaper was already rolling the second along to the ramp.

They watched it fall and crash into the sea. Then, working with the rest of the team, they quickly jettisoned the rest of the cargo out of the back of the plane until the entire aircraft was empty except for the passengers. As Reaper closed the cargo door back up, they took off their tethers and made their way back up to the cockpit. When they got there, Hawke was dumping fuel down to the bare minimum.

"We're landing in five. We'll be going straight in."

"How do we go straight in?" Kamala asked.

"Like this," said Hawke. "This is Alpha Mike Charlie Four Zero Zero Niner Two advising bingo fuel."

"Negative, I don't understand what you mean and the pattern is full."

"What's happening?" Kamala asked nervously.

"I'm being stupid," Hawke said.

"And why break the habit of a lifetime?" Scarlet said.

"Bingo fuel is military slang for being at minimum fuel and requesting a priority landing, but Half Moon Bay is a civilian airport. They think I'm just some stupid tosser pissing about."

Scarlet raised an eyebrow. "Don't we all, darling."

"Thanks for that, Cairo. I'll try again."

When Hawke clarified the situation, the tower directed him straight in on Runway 30.

"All good?" asked Scarlet. "Or are you still being an idiot?"

"All good. So belt up, Cairo," he said. "And also put your seatbelt on."

"Funny. Hilarious, even," she said as she turned and walked back into the main cabin.

Hawke wasn't listening. Yoke gripped in his left hand and right hand on the throttles, he carefully controlled the descent of the giant transporter jet. The autobrake was already set to max – hell, he wasn't paying for the rubber so why not? The runway was in sight and looking unnervingly short. He had landed a lot of planes on a lot of runways from brand new asphalt to old grass and gravel bush strips. This one was raising his heartbeat more than most. Failure meant smashing through the end of the runway and ploughing through a field toward a few dozen residential properties.

Not to mention the end of the mission.

Over the threshold and throttles to idle. The four enormous GE turbofans fell almost silent as the 380,000 pound jet crossed over the piano keys and touched down. When all twenty-eight wheels were burning rubber on the asphalt he activated the reversers. The engines roared loudly, booming across the quiet bay as the plane juddered and screeched and whined. Ahead, the end of the runway raced toward them.

"Cutting it a bit fine, Joe!" Brooke said, hands gripped on the edges of his seat.

Hawke saw the end of runway one hundred yards away, and the plane still speeding toward it. "Think of it as character building, Jack."

"If I make it out of this plane alive, I promise I will."

"The vast majority of people I have flown have survived landings."

Brooke was astonished. "Huh?"

Off the runway and into the grass, engines still roaring but now down to forty knots. "Almost there, everyone," Hawke said though the comms. More juddering and skidding and some full right rudder brought the massive airplane to a grinding, whining stop. "I'd like to thank you for flying Hawke Air, and remind you to exit the aircraft as quickly as possible. I have already sighted a nice Cessna Citation CJ4 private jet on the apron back near the ATC tower and also a rather nice helicopter that frankly looks bored just sitting there doing nothing."

Brooke's face broke into his famous crooked grin. He was clearly relieved to have survived and made it into the vast majority Hawke has just described. "You're one crazy bastard."

Hawke smiled, then turned to Alex. "How's the legs?"

She slowly got to her feet, a wide smile lighting up her face. "Better, wobbly, but better. I'll be fine in an hour or so, I think. It feels weird though."

"It's great to see," Hawke said. "Just make sure you don't overdo it."

"I won't take any chances," she said. "But I'm not hanging back like some wallflower, either."

Brooke looked concerned. "Joe's right. Just make sure you don't go too fast. Get used to it. It's a miracle, but we don't want to push our luck."

Ryan's face appeared in the cockpit door. "Our landing is already on the internet. Some nerd filmed it from one of the houses near the airport, I guess."

"Nerd, eh?" Hawke said, unbuckling his harness and climbing out of his seat.

"And the fire department is already on the way, too," Ryan said. "If we're going to borrow those aircraft you just talked about, we need to get on it right now."

"Let's do it," Hawke said. "I'll take a team to San Francisco in the chopper. Everyone else get in the

Citation and get to Chicago. From there, split up into two teams. One goes into Chicago and the other borrows another plane and goes into New York. We'll coordinate after wheels up so we can act together. Everyone ready?"

The rest of the team looked back at him in the darkness of the Galaxy's giant, black belly. Eager, brave, scared, determined. He saw it all etched on their faces.

"We're ready," Lea said. "Always are."

"You can say that again," Reaper said. "Let's end this."

"Good luck, everyone," Hawke said. "We'll meet when we've deactivated the bombs. Now, we move out."

CHAPTER TWENTY-ONE

Hawke cruised the MH-6 Little Bird helicopter along the east coast of the San Francisco Peninsula. Dogpatch, Mission Bay and South Beach flashed by beneath them in a blur and then he banked to the left and flew into the main city. Navigating a careful path through the skyscrapers and high-rise residential buildings of the Soma District, he located what he was looking for and headed over to land the stolen aircraft.

The Yerba Buena Gardens was a modest public park surrounded with trees just off to the west of the museum containing the bomb and the best place in the area to set down a chopper safely. He hovered over the grass for a few seconds and ensured no one was beneath and then lowered the collective. Seconds later, the small helicopter was touching down on the ground and he killed the engine.

Turning in his seat, he faced the others. Lexi, Alex, Zeke and Nikolai were all looking back at him, waiting for their instructions, but in their hearts they already knew what was about to happen. After stealing the helicopter back at Half Moon Bay airport, they had disabled the transponder and flown out to San Bruno Mountain State Park to hide out until the other teams were in place. Lea's team was in Chicago and Scarlet's team was in New York City after apprehending another private jet from a small regional airport on Chicago's Hanover Park. Now they were all waiting to strike.

"All right," he said, checking his battered watch. "This is it. The other two teams are in place and ready to move and it's essential we all go at the exact same time. The second Faulkner works out what's going on, he will set off the bombs remotely and it's game over, not just for us but for millions of people across America. And speaking bluntly, he could set them off at any time."

"Quite the pep talk," Lexi said, crossing her long legs and raising an eyebrow. "You're worse than Zeke."

"I'll take that as a compliment," he continued. "We can make a safe assumption his team has already worked out who trashed Half Moon Bay airport with the Galaxy. From there, it's an obvious leap that we're in the vicinity of the San Francisco bomb. He might not have worked out we split into three teams, or he might already know. Lea and Scarlet were both going to kill the transponders of any aircraft they flew in tonight, but maybe Faulkner got a satellite on them. I just can't say. From this point on we just have to take it as it comes."

"I'm ready," Zeke said. "Tonight, we make history."

Hawke nodded. "If the following words ever meant anything, they mean something right now. Failure is not an option."

To underline the point, he ended his sentence by smacking a fresh magazine into the grip of his gun and stuffing it in his holster. "It's the five of us against however many men Faulkner stationed to guard the nuke. Whatever it takes, and I mean *whatever*, we get inside that building, we kill every last man and woman working for Faulkner and then we locate the weapon. Then we disable it and pray the deactivation codes Blanchard was storing on Tartarus are valid and current. If not, we're all going into the stratosphere tonight. And that can also happen any time Davis Faulkner gets too nervous to contain himself and decides to initiate Operation Perses. That is the mission briefing. All good?"

Nods.

"Alex?"

"I'm fine," she said. "Better than ever. My legs feel stronger than ever."

"Good," he said, nodding. "But make sure you tell me if anything starts to go wrong."

"Will do."

His smile faded. "Then out we go."

Hawke stepped out of the chopper, blades still whirring above his head, and ran east across the park. Then he led the team across a smooth tiled plaza attached to an arts center before finally reaching Third Street. Checking all was clear, he made his way over the crossing and then headed for the main entrance. Walking straight past it, he headed south and then turned left down Natoma Street where they quickly reached high black gates.

Over the top and then he was running up a set of concrete steps running along the east side of the museum. He saw two doors on his left, one halfway up and the other at the top of the steps. He drew his gun and raised it into the aim. Glancing behind him, the rest followed his lead and drew their weapons. After the long flight from the island and the wait in the park, it was already stretching towards late afternoon, and their shadows were long on the steps as they made their way to the top.

Halfway up and the first door opened to reveal a man in a leather jacket. Inches from the steps, the Englishman instantly saw he was wearing an earpiece and when he reached for a holster, Hawke drew his weapon and fired into the man's chest. The report of the three shots was muffled slightly by the English commando burying the muzzle into the man's stomach when he fired, using it like a big, fat pillow to swallow the sound of the shots. The man fell back onto the floor behind him and Hawke moved to fire a double tap into his head but saw he was already dead.

"Change of plan," Hawke said. "We're going in this door, not the top one."

He stepped inside and scanned but saw no one else. The others slipped inside and he closed the door. They were standing on a metal walkway that was leading to the fire escape they had just used to enter the building. Hawke leaned down and opened the man's jacket, rummaging around until he found his wallet. Opening it, he saw what he had expected.

"US Secret Service," he said. "He got unlucky opening the door right when we were standing by it."

"Who cares?" Lexi said, kicking the dead body with the toe of her boot and staring down with contempt. "He worked for Faulkner and would have killed us all in a heartbeat. Now he's out of the game and their side is a man down."

"And we have this," Alex said, reaching down and taking the man's radio from his belt.

"Good work, Alex," Hawke said. "And we can expect a call any second."

"Why?" Nikolai asked.

"This guy didn't come out for a cigarette," Lexi said. "Use your head. He was doing his rounds. Probably has to call in every few minutes."

The radio crackled. "This is Anderson. All good where you are, Mitchell?"

Hawke took the radio from Alex. "All good, over."

"Roger that."

Alex raised an eyebrow. "Not a bad accent, Joe. Maybe a bit too *Goodfellas*, but not bad."

"Thanks, I think." He stuffed the radio into his pocket. "Now we have to find a nuclear bomb before that maniac in the White House blows this entire city to radioactive dust."

"And who says we never have any fun?" Zeke said with a wink.

"I want whatever you're smoking because this doesn't feel much like fun to me," said Alex.

Hawke readied his gun. "It's business, is what it is, and we're late to the party. Everyone follow me and keep your eyes peeled. We need to get to the weapon fast and we can't allow any more delays. We have to be in place ready for when the other teams call in. We can't be the guys holding everything up. Cairo will never let me live it down."

Zeke laughed. "I hear that, brother."

"All right, let's go!" Hawke said. "Thanks to Jack's work raiding Blanchard's office, we know the bomb's in the basement, but now they know we're here things are going to move much faster. This is our last chance to stop this thing, so let's get on it."

CHAPTER TWENTY-TWO

Lea ran up the steps of the Chicago Transit Authority metro stop at Grand station and surfaced on West Grand Avenue outside an empty Starbucks. Reaper, Kahlia and Tawan were right behind her, and weirdly, so was the President of the United States, Jack Brooke. At least the *genuine* president, she thought. She still hadn't gotten completely used to him being around, but she knew the real man, not the politician or the president, and he was both easy and good to know. That made the weirdness easier to handle.

"It's this way," Brooke said. "I know this town, and the best way to the pier is along this avenue and over the river into River North and Streeterville. The only problem is, it's too far to walk, so we're going to need some wheels."

"Know a good hire place?" Kahlia said, eyebrow raised.

"Not at this time of the evening."

She shrugged. "Just asking."

"So what do we do?" Tawan asked.

Reaper already had the answer, and was flagging a seven seater cab down. It slowed and pulled over on the side of the road.

"We need a ride to the pier," he said in his thick French accent.

The cab driver leaned closer and frowned. "What did you say, man?"

Brooke was suddenly next to the former Legionnaire. "He said we need a ride to the pier."

"Sure, got it. Get in."

They climbed in, Lea up front next to the driver and Brooke in the back with Reaper, Tawan and Kahlia. The cab driver pulled away and lowered the volume of his radio, squinting at Brooke in the mirror. "Don't I know you?"

"It's possible," Brooke said.

"Yeah… I *know* I know you from somewhere."

"He has one of those faces," Lea said.

The driver cruised over the bridge, shaking his head. With one more look in the mirror, he sucked his teeth. "That is gonna bug me all night."

"Maybe he just looks like someone you know?" Kahlia said.

The driver's face scrunched up and he shook his head. "Nah, it's more than that. I feel like I know him." He looked at Brooke one more time in the mirror. "I feel like I *know* you. Do I know you?"

"I don't think so," Brooke said with a smile.

"Wait a minute!" the driver said with snap of his fingers. "I know!"

"You do?" Lea asked.

"Sure I do. I met you at Dolores's wedding, right?"

Brooke smiled. "You got me."

The driver laughed as he steered the cab through the city. "I knew I'd get it in the end."

Brooke's smile faded. The game with the cab driver was over and all that remained was the horror of tracking down the hidden nuke. The fact Chicago was still on the planet was more luck than judgement, he thought unnervingly.

Lea turned away from the driver and looked at her watch. The sands of time were running out faster than any of them could have ever dared imagine. With the seconds ticking by, she prayed Hawke and Scarlet and their teams were in place and ready to make the call to deactivate the nuke. The Navy Pier was less than five minutes away now and soon they would be on the final leg of their journey. Letting the other teams down was not an option she could live with. Looking up at Brooke she saw he was thinking the exact same thing.

"Don't worry," he said reassuringly. "We'll be there on time."

"I hope so, Jack. Time's getting on."

"You'll get there on time!" the driver said. "I know this town better than anyone else. All the short cuts and all the tricks. Dolores taught me. Best cab driver in Mud City. We'll be at the pier in four minutes."

"Thank God for Dolores," Lea muttered, and turned to watch the innocent faces of the pedestrians as they walked along the sidewalks, totally oblivious of the terrible threat hanging over their city.

CHAPTER TWENTY-THREE

No matter how many times she saw it, the New York City skyline never stopped impressing Scarlet Sloane. Tonight, the city's lights sparkled in the distance as she cruised their hired SUV across the Brooklyn Bridge. Stealing a Daher-Socata TBM from the small airfield outside of Chicago had been easy enough with such light security and the powerful turboprop had made the journey in a little under ninety minutes. Slipping through JFK with the false passports provided by Orlando Sooke was even faster.

Now, leaving the East River behind them, she pulled off the bridge and headed down FDR Drive, her head spinning with all the possible outcomes a night like this might provide. Murder and mayhem, for sure, but the spectre of nuclear apocalypse was something else altogether. Something that made her feel sick to the pit of her stomach.

In the neon streets of the city, she turned right onto Broad Street and drove the Chevy north into Manhattan, crossing Wall Street before turning a final left on Nassau. With a nervous sigh, she pulled to a stop on the sidewalk in front of one of the large metal security barriers in position at either end of the famous eight-block street.

"We're here, kids."

Ryan turned to Kamala. "You know this city?"

"Not really," she said with a shrug. "You probably know it better than I do."

"A little," Ryan said.

Scarlet was checking her gun. "I don't think playing on GTA 5 fifty hours a week counts, boy."

"I've spent some time in the *real* city, too, Cairo," he said, turning to Ravi. "What about you?"

"Not at all, friend. When we are in Rio, then talk to me. I know that city better than anyone in the world. Here, I am a fish out of water."

"It doesn't matter," Scarlet said coolly. "Not unless we get separated."

"And then we meet back at the car," Ravi said. "Right?"

Kamala laughed. "I might not know New York too well, but I know this car ain't going to be here by the time we get back. It's parked way too close to the Stock Exchange. Anti-terror cops will be all over it."

"If we get split up," Scarlet said, "We meet down in The Battery, it's a park on the southern tip of Manhattan. Even Ryan could find it. And stay out of sight when you're in there. We'll do a Major Hawke after that and make it up as we go along."

"Sounds good to me," Ryan said.

Scarlet glanced at her watch. All right, listen up. Hawke and Lea and their teams are all in position and zero hour is in less than five minutes. Hawke's already inside the museum. We drew the short straw, because the New York Stock Exchange has some of the chunkiest security in the city, much more than museums or piers."

Ryan grinned. "Bitter?"

"Are you kidding? I live for challenges like this. The museum in San Francisco probably has the security of a childcare center."

Ryan chuckled. "Funny, but I don't know about that. Remember, Faulkner's goons will be at all three locations, and they mean serious business."

"Good," Scarlet said icily. "Because I like serious business. Now, get the kit out of the trunk and follow me. All of you. We're going in the tradesman's entrance."

"Said the bishop to the actress!" said Ryan, nudging Scarlet in the ribs. "C'mon, admit it. That was funny."

"Grow up, Ryan."

He opened his door. "Only if I have to."

"How are we getting in?" Kamala asked.

"Through the roof," said Scarlet. "Any objections."

"Don't look at me," Ravi said smoothly. "I once broke into a bank in Santa Teresa through the roof. To me, this is like child's play."

"Then let's move out," Scarlet said.

Behind her, Ravi and Kamala were already opening their doors. When they were all outside, Ryan looked up at the massive skyscraper jutting up into the sky behind the Stock Exchange. The very top was obscured by low cloud, lit orange by the warm glow of the enormous city's nightlife.

"It's time to play Spiderman!" he said, rubbing his hands together.

Scarlet huffed out a cold laugh. "Spiderwoman, please darling."

*

The view from the fifteenth floor of the skyscraper directly behind the Stock Exchange would have been breathtaking, were it not for a thick band of rain that had blown in as they ascended the building in one of the maintenance elevators. Now, standing on a ledge at the front of the building, Scarlet was carefully studying the view ahead of them of the NYSE's roof for somewhere to aim her grappling hook.

"And I think we have our place," she said quietly. "Aircon unit on the right hand side of the lower roof. We go there."

Ravi sighed. "When you said we would be going in through the roof, I didn't think that meant sliding across on a rope from a building on the other side of the street."

"Welcome to ECHO," Kamala said with a shrug. "This is sort of how we do business."

He peered down at the rain soaked street far below. "It seems sort of… risky."

"Going in through any of the main or side entrances is *risky*," Scarlet said. "Not only does each one have some of the highest security in New York, but tonight they're going to have Faulkner's men in there too. Talk about poking a bees' nest."

"Wonder what they think they're guarding?" Ryan said. "Sure as hell can't be a nuke or they wouldn't be anywhere near the place."

"They wouldn't question him," Kamala said. "They're Secret Service and he's the president. What he says, kinda goes. If he told them to guard these locations, they would do it. That's their oath-sworn duty. Or, he may even have told them they were guarding them in preparation for a presidential visit at some point in the next day or so. Any number of ways he could have these guys out here tonight without them knowing the truth, if that's the way he wanted to play it."

"You think if we told them the truth they'd come onto our side?" Ryan said.

Scarlet laughed.

"I doubt it," Kamala said. "Although seeing the actual bomb might change their minds. These guys are not stupid."

"Unfortunately, I doubt they'll get the chance to see it," Scarlet said. "Because the only way we can get anywhere near it will be taking them out first and we have no time to mess about with a Q&A session in the meantime. C'mon, we're going in!"

Scarlet led the way, climbing into her harness and fixing her carabiner to the zip line. With a devilish wink back at her team, she launched herself forward and was instantly away from the building, zipping along the line hundreds of feet above Manhattan.

She touched down lightly on the Stock Exchange's roof and signaled for the rest of the team to come over. Ravi was next, followed by Kamala and then Ryan at the rear. When the team was safely gathered on the roof and out of their harnesses, Scarlet drew her gun and walked over to a concrete bulkhead on the other side of the rain-blasted roof.

"It's in here," she said, aiming her gun at the lock. She fired once and blew the lock to pieces.

"Nice shooting," Ravi said.

Inside, Scarlet led the way down some concrete steps to another door. This time it was open and revealed a long corridor lined with doors.

"Any idea which way goes down to the trading floor?" Ryan asked.

"Don't look at me," Kamala said.

"Nor me," said Ravi with a sheepish grin. "But it's going to be exciting to find out, no?"

"Exciting or deadly," Scarlet said.

They made their way down the corridor, kicking open doors until they found another set of steps. This time they were varnished wood and not concrete, and the walls were lined with large monotone photographs of New York's most famous landmarks. Doors opened onto plush wooden boardrooms, one of which was much more impressive than the others.

"This must be the Executive Floor," Ryan said. "I watched a documentary on this place once and this looks like the main conference room."

Scarlet peered inside and saw various historical objects and a large glass case on the wall full of Civil War bonds. An antique grandfather clock added yet more class to the opulent room and not far from its varnished case was an original Andy Warhol artwork and, in the far corner, a beautiful, varnished electric guitar.

"What the hell is that doing here?" she asked.

Ryan grinned. "It's one of Jimmy Page's Les Paul guitars. You know, from Led Zeppelin."

She gave him a withering glance. "I *know*, but I don't care," she said.

"But they were *your* era," he said with a wink.

"Get screwed."

"Is that an offer?"

"Only in your dreams."

They made their way down a staircase whose walls were covered in hundreds of autographs.

"What are all these for, Ryan?" Kamala asked.

"They're the signatures of everyone who has ever visited the stock exchange to ring the opening and closing bell."

"Yawn," said Scarlet, gun gripped firmly in her hand. "And can we please keep our minds on the job instead of indulging the walking history channel behind us."

"Hey!" Ryan said.

The stairs turned halfway on a wide landing and then revealed another door. When they opened it, they found themselves in the main trading floor of the NYSE. Scanning for guards and soldiers, they stepped out into the massive space in awe. Trading desks arranged in islands and giant viewing screens were everywhere they looked. On the far wall was the marble balcony with the world-famous bell in front of it. Here was where the world's economy woke up every morning and went back to sleep every night. The market capitalization of all its listed companies was over twenty-one trillion dollars and every single day, nearly one hundred and seventy billion dollars was traded here.

"Start looking for the bomb," Scarlet said. "Our intel says it's on this floor.

Between the four of them, the search didn't take long. It turned out Faulkner's men had positioned it inside one of the trading desk islands in the center of the floor, innocuously tucked away inside a large metal crate with a padlock on top of it.

"I have it!" Ryan said. Drawing his gun, he blew the padlock off and swung open the crate's heavy metal lid.

"My God," Ravi said nervously. "So this is a nuclear bomb?"

"Sorry, but yes." Ryan said nonchalantly.

"You don't seem very frightened," he said.

"It's not my first time."

Ravi considered the hideous creation right in front of him. "What about radiation. Aren't we all getting exposed to dangerous levels just by standing here?"

"I never thought of that," Kamala said with a shudder.

"No, we're not," Ryan said. "The dangerous part is behind massive shielding, but only until the detonation. Then it's, well… *everywhere*."

"In that case, we had better make sure it doesn't detonate, no?" the Brazilian said with a nervous smile.

"Ravi's right, Ryan," Kamala said, glancing at her watch. "We'd better make a start."

"And when you say *we*, you do of course mean *me*," said Ryan with a cocky head-wobble.

"She does," Scarlet said. "Now get on it before I give you a slap, cock knocker."

Ryan ignored the insult and went straight to work, carefully unscrewing a heavy black steel panel on top of the bomb's outer casing. He lifted it off and handed it to Ravi, who laid it gently beside the crate the bomb was in.

"What do you think?" Scarlet asked.

"I can do it," he said. "But the place you type the deactivation code looks like it's behind some kind of booby trap."

"Shit, I never thought of that," Scarlet said. "How long?"

"Not long. I just need to open up the section under these wires and find the foul, beating heart of the beast."

"Is that dangerous?" Kamala asked, peering over his shoulder as he worked. He slowly untangled and cut various wires until he was able to lift a small steel plate out of the way to reveal what they were looking for.

"Maybe," he said, and started rummaging around inside the tangle of wires. After a few moments of cursing and muttering, his face lit up. "I've got it! I'm just putting the deactivation code into it now." He typed it in and a small metal cylinder clicked above the smooth level of the bomb's casing. He reached down and grabbed it. "I've got the neutron trigger. It's over."

Scarlet suppressed a long sigh of relief. "Good work, boy."

"Thanks. Glad to hear I've been promoted from cock knocker back up to boy again."

Ignoring him, Scarlet peered inside the tangle of wires and circuit boards. "Now mess that thing up so it'll never work again."

"There's no need if we've got the trigger."

"And what if the Psycho-in-Chief sends more of his goons over here with a spare trigger?"

"Ah."

She took the trigger from him and slapped him around the back of his head with her gloved hand. "Now mess it up, like I just told you."

"Got it," he said, tearing at the wires and ramming the grip of his gun down onto the circuit boards. "Consider it truly messed up."

"Even better work," she said. "Now, we need to get out of here. Everyone, go!"

As the team made their way back to the door, Scarlet stayed behind for a second and stared down at the monstrous weapon. It seemed to return her gaze with its own malevolent stare and gave her a shudder down her spine. When she turned to catch up with the rest of her team, she heard shouting and boots pounding on the trading room floor.

"Freeze!" a man yelled.

It happened as fast as lightning. Countless men, some in black Special Ops fatigues, others dressed in suits she guessed were US Secret Service agents. One of them opened fire on her team and sent them scattering for cover all over the large trading floor. Bullets ricocheted off desks and shattered the giant viewing screens above Scarlet's head. She dived to the floor and rolled inside one of the trading desk islands in the middle of the vast floor. Pulling her palm mic up to her mouth with one hand, she pushed her back up against the desk and swept her gun along the area behind her to make sure she was safe. She was, but only for now.

"This is Cairo," she said into the mic. "You guys all right?"

"I'm fine," Ravi said, replying first, his Brazilian accent weak in the crackling static. "I'm under one of the desks about twenty meters away from you."

“I’m good too,” Ryan said. “I’m further to Ravi’s right and I can see them fanning out all over the place. Some of them are even up on the balcony with the bell on it.”

“All right,” Scarlet said. “And Kamala?”

Static.

“Kamala?”

“I’m hit…” said a weak voice. “They got me in the upper arm. It’s just a flesh wound, I think, but it’s bleeding and it hurts like hell. I’m going to try and rip some cloth from my shirt and use it as some kind of tourniquet. I need you guys to keep them busy while that happens.”

“Count on it,” Scarlet said. “You heard her, guys. Let’s take this party up a notch. And Ryan, for *buggery’s* sake do not let any of them get their hands on that trigger.”

“I *pwomise* mummy.”

“It’s serious time, boy.”

His voice was suddenly all business. “Don’t worry, Cairo. I’ve got it. You can rely on me.”

Scarlet lowered wrist and peered over the desk. A bullet instantly struck the surface a few inches from her eyes with a puff of dust and blasted off behind her head, burying itself in the TV screen behind her. *This is going to be interesting*, she thought.

Interesting and lethal.

And then, in the chaos of gunfire and screams, she heard a voice she recognized. Someone screaming. Someone in pain.

Ravi Monteiro, the new guy.

CHAPTER TWENTY-FOUR

In San Francisco, Zeke sprinted down the stairs with as much speed as he could muster without stumbling. A short exchange of gunfire with a mix of US Secret Service and museum security had ended in the deaths of several of the guards and one USSS agent. The ECHO team had almost taken a fatality when a ricocheting bullet nearly hit Lexi in the chest. After that, they had moved like lightning down to the basement.

Now, with his hands gripped on the rail, the Texan descended into the basement with his long stride eating up three of the concrete steps at a time and hit the bottom running. What was down here, he had yet to discover – maybe more armed men, a boobytrap, some kind of IED… but none of that was about to stop him. As the most experienced person in the sub-unit in bomb disposal, his teammates and the rest of San Francisco were relying on him to get to the bomb and deactivate it with the codes Brooke had taken from Blanchard's office.

Lexi Zhang was right behind him, jumping from the third step up and smacking down on the polished concrete a few paces to his left like a wildcat. She swept the dimly lit room with her gun and called out all clear and was then followed by Alex and Nikolai. Hawke had been delayed in the fire fight up top in the museum, but was now beside them, gun in hand.

"All right, now we start looking," Hawke said. "Thanks to the files Jack got back on Tartarus, we know it's in here somewhere, but no precise location. Get going."

Zeke was already looking at the job in hand. The museum's basement was vast and mostly used as a storage facility for any items of art or sculpture not currently on display on one of the floors above. Some of the larger *objets d'art* were out for all to see – a giant bronze sculpture of a prancing horse, a white marble carving of Sagittarius, a massive replica of the Earth, but most were under dust sheets or in countless boxes, sealed and lined up into aisles leading down into the darkness.

"Holy crap, Joe!" Lexi said. "There must be a hundred boxes in here and the bomb could be in any one of them. We don't even have a damned Geiger counter. That would make this easy."

"I count less than that – maybe seventy or eighty boxes," Alex said. "I think we can do it, if we all work fast."

The big Texan scanned down one of the aisles, squinting as he made his own quick count of the inventory. "Me too."

"They're right," Nikolai said. "That's only around fifteen or sixteen each."

"Then let's get to work," said Hawke. "And we can get started by pulling all these dust sheets off. No sense prising open dozens of boxes if the damn thing is just under one of these."

He started proceedings by tearing a large cloth dust sheet from an angular shape to his right to reveal a grotesque modern art sculpture of a nude with three heads.

"Yikes," Alex said.

"Each to their own," Lexi said. "Some people have taste, and others have… *this*."

Hawke laughed, then he began his search for the bomb in the boxes lined up against the wall on their right. Alex was in the row beside him, then Lexi and Nikolai and then

Zeke was on the left, checking the boxes running along the other wall just below the steps they had used to enter the basement.

As the Texan tank commander prised off lid after lid and fumbled through the contents in search of the mini nuke, he felt the pressure rising inside him. Yes, he had some basic training in bomb deactivation and disposal but not nuclear. His knowledge was mostly limited to deactivating IEDs found out in the field, many of which were used to disable tanks like the one he had commanded in Iraq.

But this was different. Even with the deactivation codes, if he couldn't make sense of the nuclear device hidden in this room, then he would die tonight, along with his friends and probably well over a million people. More, if the blast were bigger than expected and reached out across the Bay Area, there would be all the fallout deaths over the next few years. It was the gift from hell that never stopped giving.

And entirely down to him whether it worked its evil or not.

Sixth box… *empty.*

Seventh box… *empty.*

Maybe Blanchard had lied to Brooke. Maybe the files with the locations were fakes – designed to throw them off the scent. Maybe the bomb was somewhere else. San Francisco was a big city. Endless districts and streets and alleyways and trashcans and sewer pipes and roof spaces to hide a mini nuke in. As he tore open the last box in his line, he felt an acute sense of hopelessness engulf him. Just like all the other boxes, there was nothing in it except small sculptures, ornaments, pottery, ceramics, some oil paintings on canvas neatly stacked against the side.

No mini nuke.

His heart beat faster, sweat beaded on his forehead. For the first time since he had met ECHO, he wondered if he had done the right thing in joining them in their quest against men like the Athanatoi and Davis Faulkner. Then he heard Alex call out some magical words.

"Guys, I got it!"

He ran toward her, catching up with Lexi and Nikolai on the way. Hawke was already standing beside the American woman, peering down into the box, wincing. "That ain't pretty," he said.

"No, it sure ain't," Alex said.

"But can you stop it, Zeke?" asked Nikolai.

Zeke took a deep breath. He knew he had to inspire confidence in the team, no matter how nervous he felt. "Count me in as hell to the yeah, baby!"

Showtime.

He looked down into the box and saw the mini nuke. Hawke was right – it was a small, ugly thing, almost boxlike in appearance but with slightly curved edges making it vaguely resemble a large, black metal American football. The main housing was bolted together with chunky rivets and a small panel was on the top with a line of red digital zeroes on it.

"The timer isn't set," he said.

"Remember, Blanchard told my Dad that Faulkner would detonate the bombs remotely if things got desperate enough," Alex said. "So I hate to say it, but this could go off at any second."

"A timer counting down would be easier to handle," Lexi said grimly. "At least then we would have some kind of idea of the time we had left."

"Exactly," added Nikolai. "This way, it could blow up in our faces at any time and we have no way of knowing when."

"Whoa," Hawke said. "Enough of the morale boosting, everyone! Let's just get to work and deactivate the weapon. That's all we have to focus on right now, just like Lea and Cairo's teams will be doing."

Zeke agreed and reached into his pack and pulled out the toolbox they had taken from the helicopter. "Okay boys and girls, this is it – party time. If I can't do this, we're riding this baby all the way to the moon."

As the others exchanged nervous glances, Ezekiel Jones leaned down to the bomb, muttered a silent prayer and went to work for maybe the last time in his life.

CHAPTER TWENTY-FIVE

Kahlia was buzzing. It was crazy, she knew. After all, she was running headlong into a nuclear bomb that could go off at any second. But she was still buzzing. A few hours ago she was staring down the barrel of an indeterminate prison sentence in Tartarus, mostly in solitary confinement. Despite what she thought in the dark times, she had never given up hope of getting out one day, but she had figured she would probably be a little old lady by the time that happened.

But now she was free as a bird and sprinting down Chicago's Navy Pier with some pretty cool people, people she thought she could spend some serious time with. Maybe even become friends with. Lea was nice. Tough but kind and had a good sense of humor. The French guy was almost a walking cliché with his height and muscles and stubble and *that accent…* The guy from Thailand was a mystery, but strong and brave.

Oh yeah, and then there was her latest friend, President Jack Brooke. The last time she had seen him was on TV before her arrest in Hawaii. He was standing in the Oval Office shaking hands with the French President and discussing some kind of trans-Atlantic trade deal. Now he was running down the pier not five feet from her.

Life comes at you fast, Keahi, she thought.

She ran harder. Night was all around them now. Stars sparkled in the sky and a cool breeze drifted off Lake Michigan. She felt like she was nineteen again, running out to catch her first wave with a surfboard under her arm and the whole of her life stretching out in front of her, fading into the blue haze of the ocean beyond.

Except she was getting further away from nineteen every day, and there was no ocean. Tonight it was the lake. And the beach was the pier, hosting a few dozen people strolling around with their hands in their pockets. The surfboard was gone too, but she was packing an M18 modular handgun that she had liberated from one of the dead USAF guards back on the island.

Yeah, life sure does come at you fast.

They continued on their way to the Centennial Wheel, an enormous Ferris wheel stretching nearly two hundred feet into the night sky. Inside one of those enclosed gondolas was Faulkner's gift to the people of Chicago, a small mini nukc rcady to blast the entire city into the dark ages, and only she and her new friends knew it was there.

And the men guarding it.

She scanned for them. Lea, Reaper, Tawan and Jack Brooke were on her flanks, already doing the same as her, with their hands floating perilously close to the concealed sidearms under their jackets.

"I count at least three," Lea said. "All wearing leather jackets and milling around the base of the Ferris wheel."

"And I see a fourth," said Reaper. "The short guy in the denim jacket pretending to choose a hotdog from that little cart."

"And the guy behind the cart," Brooke said. "Any regular vendor would be suspicious of someone hanging around like that and not buying. They're not even talking." They got closer. "And now I see they're both wearing earpieces."

"So that's at least five," Tawan said.

"Let's take a quick tour of the pier first," Lea said. "And see if there are any more. Keep your face out of sight, Jack. We don't want another cab driver moment where you get recognized."

"Are you sure it's not just because you don't like my face?"

She smiled. "Pretty sure."

They made their way along the footpath behind the hotdog cart, hands in pockets and as casual as anyone else. When the man in the denim jacket looked over at them, Lea linked her arm through Reaper's and kissed him on the cheek. Brooke turned away and pretended to look out across the lake. Then, Kahlia slipped her arm around his waist and kissed him on the cheek too.

"Sorry Mr President," she said smoothly. "It's just to improve our cover, you understand."

The former soldier grinned. "Sure it is, and good thinking, Miss Keahi. What were you in prison for again?"

"A charm offensive, sir."

He chuckled. "Well, good work. Our hungry friend has turned back around and is looking at his menu again."

"Those hotdogs must be *fascinating*," Lea said.

Down to the end of the pier and back again, walking alongside East Grand Avenue. Quiet tonight, Kahlia noticed. Maybe, not for long. She followed Lea along the pier until they reached the east side of the Centennial Wheel and steeled herself for trouble.

"It's in the Wheel," Lea said. "All the agents are stationed around the Wheel."

"Agreed," Brooke said, reaching into his pocket and pulling Blanchard's personal M9 pistol gun into the night. "And now it's time to act."

"Nice weapon," Kahlia said. "That'll blow a hole through the merc and the merc standing behind the merc, too. Cool."

"Thanks, but it's not mine," he said with a frown. "The base commander at Tartarus left it to me in his will."

"Gotcha."

"I think they saw us," Reaper said. "Head's up."

"They did!" Tawan called out, pointing at the hotdog cart. "He's taking cover behind the cart and firing!"

"Cover!" Lea yelled, and the team scattered. "Now!"

Brooke and Tawan went down behind a corrugated storage unit. Reaper was further ahead and now dived for cover alongside Lea behind the base of one of the Centennial Wheel's heavy duty support struts.

Lea crashed into the artificial turf, staring up at the US Secret Service guards taking up defensive positions around the west side of the wheel. She counted at least one under the pagoda directly beneath the Ferris wheel, taking cover behind a concrete barrier and some box hedging. She thought fast. The problem was that even after taking the guards out and reaching the Wheel, they still had no idea where inside it the mini nuke was hidden, and if these guys radioed into base about the attack, Faulkner might order the detonation at any second.

"I'm making a break for the southside of the pier," Brooke said over the comms. "We need to come at them from more than one direction to stand any chance at all."

"Got it," Lea said.

Brooke broke cover and sprinted across the pier, using a large marquee for cover before slamming down behind a closed falafel stand a few dozen yards east of the hotdog cart. Both the agents there now turned and opened fire on him, their rounds punching dozens of holes up and down the steel walls of the mobile falafel trailer. The handful of tourists still milling around now screamed and ran along the pier back to the shore.

"You okay?" Reaper said through the comms.

"I'm fine," Brooke said. "The rounds aren't getting through this side of the stand, but now they're heading toward me!"

"Not for lor long, Mr President," Kahlia said, breaking cover and running under the covered area toward the stand. As she sprinted, the tattooed young woman held her gun out at arm's length and fired half a dozen pot shots at the agents, striking one of them in the chest and blasting him to the floor, dead.

With the guard in the hotdog vendor apron now opening fire on Kahlia, Brooke leaned around the side of the falafel stand and aimed Blanchard's M9 at him. He fired a shot and took half his head off just as Kahlia skidded to a halt beside him.

Gunshots in the background, a man screaming. Tourists sprinting for the safety of the shore.

"Whoa, that was a better rush than the Banzai Pipeline!"

He looked at her, confused. "Huh?"

"Big wave off Oahu North Shore. Deadliest in the world, but I never got shot at by US Secret Service agents before."

"I'm sorry you had to go through it, Kahlia," he said. "But it looks like I owe you big time."

"I'll think of something, sir. Maybe a presidential pardon and two million dollars compensation?"

"Don't push your life, Keahi!"

Another peel of gunshots ahead of them. Kahlia looked around the stand and saw Lea, Reaper and Tawan storming the pagoda at the base of the Wheel. Off to the left, they saw two more of the guards dead, sprawled out on the pier's boardwalk.

"They're going in!" she said.

"And so are we!" Brooke got up and reached his hand down to help her to her feet. "Let's get going."

She followed Brooke up the pier until they reached the Wheel, just in time to see Reaper killing the last guard in the pagoda. As his bullet-shredded body slumped to the floor, Lea leaped over him and ran into the Ferris Wheel's control room.

"The nuke is in one of these gondolas," she said hurriedly. "It has to be. If I turn it on and bring it round one gondola at a time, we can check each one here at the base."

"Which is not as fun as climbing up and jumping from gondola to gondola," Kahlia said.

"Which is not as *insane* as climbing up and jumping from gondola to gondola," said Lea. "And also much quicker. Jack, you and Kahlia and Tawan set up a defensive perimeter to the west and check for backup. Me and Reaper will go through the gondolas. He's the best bomb disposal guy we have on the team."

"Consider it done," Brooke said, turning to Kahlia and Tawan. "C'mon! Let's do it."

Lea and Reaper were alone in the quiet darkness, lit now only by the emergency lighting of the Ferris Wheel's control room. "I count forty-two gondolas, Reap. We'd better get going." Slowly, she operated the machine and brought each gondola to the base where they both went inside and searched under the seats.

Inside Gondola twenty-three they finally found what they were looking for, and she radioed it across to Brooke's forward team outside. "We got it, Jack. A big ugly bastard stuffed under the seats in the twenty-third gondola."

Thank God... Lea heard Kahlia mutter.

"Is it on a timer?" he asked.

"No, but there *is* a timer panel. I guess it just goes off whenever Faulkner sends the signal."

"And that's only likely if he got word we're here," Brooke said.

"Well *someone* got word all right," Kahlia said. "I see a warship coming in real fast across the lake from the north."

"A warship?" Tawan said. "On Lake Michigan?"

"Sure," Brooke said. "The US Navy trains out here all the time. They must have been in the area and got a call from someone about us. Whatever's going on, we can deduce either Faulkner doesn't want to detonate his little surprise yet or news of our presence here hasn't quite reached his level yet."

Lea turned and looked through the control room window. "Damn it! That thing is going so fast it must be almost skimming the surface of the lake!"

"It's a *Freedom*-class littoral combat ship," Brooke said. "I recognize it now. Top speed of over fifty miles per hour."

"It's firing!" Reaper said. "Look at the flashes on its deck."

"Take cover!"

CHAPTER TWENTY-SIX

Ravi Monteiro felt another bullet rip through his leather jacket and heard it ping off the air-conditioning unit's metal casing a few inches to his right. An instinctive scream burst from his lips and he cursed, feeling his heart pounding hard in his chest. He was no stranger to disagreements in the favelas of his youth, but he had never been shot at with a high-powered assault rifle after landing on the roof of a skyscraper via a zipline hundreds of feet above a busy street.

Not a bit of it.

He had never broken into a building as important as the New York Stock Exchange before.

Nowhere near.

He had never engaged in a fire fight with the US Secret Service before.

Not even close.

His wars and battles were fought out on the streets of Rio, like a panther, not above them like a hawk or an eagle. He had never used a zipline before in his life. The story about breaking into the bank in Santa Teresa that night had been a web of lies spun out to the Englishwoman to save face. That had worked, he thought, but it still didn't save him from the zipline.

I mean, just who the hell are these people?

He heard the Englishwoman's voice on the comms.

"You all right, Newbie?"

He fumbled with the palm mic, never having used one before, and adjusted the small plastic receiver in his ear. "I am okay. Thanks, Cairo."

“What happened?” she asked.

“Some bullets wandered a little too close to me, that is all. I’m fine, but I might need a new leather jacket.”

“There’ll be plenty of time for that later,” she said. “Just keep your head down and your arse in.”

Even in the carnage, he smiled. “I can do that.”

He said it, but he didn’t want to do it. Covering his behind and keeping his head down weren’t in his style. True, what was happening in here tonight was out of his league, but only because he had never fought in this league before. After tonight, he’d either be dead or *in* this league, but only if he pulled his own weight and proved he could do it, not just to Scarlet Sloane and the team but to himself.

He knew what he had to do. Turning, he leaned his arms on the desk and aimed at the approaching agents. He fired on them, taking one out and making the others scramble for the closest available cover. When in their new defensive positions, they fired back with their compact machine pistols, sending him scurrying back under the desk. Bullets flew everywhere, smashing the giant plasma trading screen above his head and showering him with shattered glass and plastic.

It was a formidable display of aggression from both the soldiers and the US Secret Service agents and almost made him turn on his heel and flee. Then he remembered what he had just told himself about proving his place on the team. He heard their footfall as they broke cover and ran toward him. He had no choice but to return fire and he did it with a fury he never knew he had inside him.

Out from under the desk again and gun swinging into the aim. He was alarmed to see how close they were but he fired again, taking careful aim and striking another of them, this time a woman. The round tore into her throat and he felt a pang of guilt – worse, nausea – as she spun around and crashed to the floor, leaving a misty cloud of blood hanging in the air where her head had been half a second before. What could be the justification for taking a life like this?

She was dead, and so was the other man he had already shot. Both of their bloody bodies lay still on the smooth, shiny floor of the exchange, guns still in their hands. But this was no time for remorse; the other agents had taken cover but were now charging his position with rage on their faces. They raised their guns and unloaded their mags at him, shredding the desk to pieces and forcing him to scuttle away to the next island along.

He heard more gunshots, this time from his side. In his new position inside the next island, he peered through a gap in the screens and saw Scarlet and Ryan firing on thc men. They hit another two and put them on the floor. One was dead but the other was only wounded. His moans broke through the mayhem now and then, but Ravi's focus was on saving his own life as the surviving agents sprinted toward him.

He tried to fire, but he was out of rounds. Ryan had given him a spare magazine but it was in his jacket pocket. He reached around and grabbed it and then tried to put it in the gun before he'd ejected the old one. Heart thumping. Hands shaking. It was chaos. He started to panic. Maybe this was no place for a thief from the favelas after all. The agents were almost at his position. He scanned for help but Scarlet and Ryan were busily engaging with men on the other side of the trading floor. He ejected the magazine and fumbled the other one, dropping it on the floor with a smack.

He cursed and reached down for it, reaching it just in time. He snatched it up and slid it inside the grip just the way Scarlet had shown him, but it was too late. One of the agents vaulted over the desk and spun around, compact machine pistol in her hands. Ravi stared into the big, ugly muzzle and hurriedly muttered a prayer in his native Portuguese. He heard gunshots and jumped, believing himself to be dead.

But he was alive, and when he opened his eyes he saw the female Secret Service agent dead on her back, gun still in her hand. He spun around and saw a heavily wounded Kamala Banks with a smoking gun in her hand. She had broken cover from her island to get the shot she needed to shoot the woman before she could kill him.

"My God, you saved my…"

The brutal, mechanical roar of an MP5 filled the vast room, and Ravi watched helplessly as bullets tore into Kamala, punching holes in her legs, torso, neck and head and sending her staggering violently backwards before collapsing in a dead, bloody heap on the floor in front of the island.

"Oh, my God!" he called out, desperate, panicked. He didn't know what to do. He gripped his gun and tucked himself away behind the desk. Grateful Kahlia couldn't see him now, cowering, he pulled the comms up to his quivering lips, he spoke to anyone who would listen.

"It's Kamala! Anyone? She is dead! I saw them kill her right in front of me… I think I'm going to be sick."

Static, then Scarlet's voice as cold as ice. "I saw it too, Ravi."

"So what do I do?"

"Sit tight, like I told you, and leave the rest to me."

"You can handle all these agents?"

"Watch me."

CHAPTER TWENTY-SEVEN

On the Californian coast, Zeke broke open the panel and stared into a mess of tangled wires. Red, blue, green – some black others yellow. Most were protruding from some kind of plastic junction box but from there, they mostly went to different locations. Some went inside the main housing, others twisted around and disappeared beneath the plastic box.

"All right, guys," he drawled, "Looks like some kind of booby trap to stop me getting to the deactivation section."

"Yeah," Lexi said. "We should have thought of that."

Hawke shrugged. "Can't think of everything."

Zeke whistled. "I'm going in. Wish me luck."

"Wait," Lexi said. "Is this one of those bombs where if you cut the wrong one, it blows up anyway?"

"Yes and no," Zeke said firmly. "First, nukes ain't really like that. A nuke has to be triggered in a certain way, by making an atom absorb neutrons. A separate explosion cannot set off a nuclear bomb. On the other hand, if this device is rigged so cutting the wrong wire causes the chain reaction early, then yes, it will blow up anyway. Hope that helps."

"Not really," Lexi said, glowering at him.

"Yeah." Alex frowned. "Not *at all*."

"Sorry, guys," Zeke muttered. "I just need some peace and quiet and some time to think and…"

The first bullet struck the wooden storage box next to Zeke and punched a hole right through it and out of the other side. It ricocheted off the wall behind them and vanished into the basement's darkness with a ghostly whine.

"What the hell!" Lexi said, spinning with her gun.

"Backup," Hawke said. "One of the agents must have got an SOS off on their radio."

"Holy crap, Joe!" Zeke said, ducking to avoid another shot. "I can't work like this… not under fire, man!"

"You think it's worth telling these guys how much danger they're in?" Nikolai said.

"Maybe," Alex said. "I doubt they're into suicide missions, even for Faulkner."

Hawke said nothing. Instead, he raised his gun and fired on the agents, taking out two of them instantly and sending the third ducking down behind the banisters. A short exchange of fire ended when the man tried to scramble back up the steps, palm mic to his lips. Hawke fired again, striking him in the head with a bullet right through the temple. As the man's dead body rolled down the steps, Hawke turned to the Texan.

"Any luck?"

"Yeah, I think so. I got through the booby trap and just entered the deactivation code. Any second now I'm expecting to see…" A metal cylinder slid up outside of the casing, allowing him to grab hold of it. He gave the team a big toothy smile. "The neutron trigger. It's time for us to fly."

*

The journey back to the helicopter was tense and grim, but at least they had the trigger and the bomb was deactivated. They strapped themselves in quickly and were soon airborne, but the celebrations were rapidly cut short when Lexi noticed other aircraft rising into view ahead of them.

Hawke followed her pointing finger ahead and just off to the left and saw several black gunships rising out of the San Francisco skyline. Leaning further over instrument panel, he peered harder into the early evening sky. "I count three of them. They're closing in on us fast."

"And three Apaches versus one Little Bird ain't much of a fair fight," said Alex. "This shit's getting real in about thirty seconds, Joe."

"I know, Alex. I've got it."

Hawke readied himself for the airborne chase of his life. On one side, himself, Alex, Lexi, Nikolai and Zeke in a light, unarmed helicopter. On the other side, three professional military crews riding in the most dangerous attack choppers ever designed. Yeah, this was going to be interesting, to say the least.

"Hold on to your hats, everyone," he said. "We're going in."

From her seat beside him, Alex now turned and gave him a look of horror. "What do you mean, 'going in'?"

Hawke twisted the collective and pushed down on it, reducing power and making the chopper descend down past the skyscrapers now screeching past them on both sides. As the road below raced up to meet them, it felt like they were flying through a valley of steel and concrete. Windows flashed past them, some lit, some dark.

Hawke flew lower still, finally bringing the aircraft level just above the height of the streetlights. Alex turned in her seat and put the window down. Looking behind them, she gasped and turned back to Hawke. "Okay, all three of the Apaches are still on our tail and closing fast."

"What altitude?" Hawke asked.

Her answer was instant. "One level with us, next one hundred feet above and the third is flying level with the top of the skyscrapers."

Hawke nodded. "Makes sense. The highest one is the surveillance. They'll be keeping an eye on us and communicating everything we do to the other two."

"Surely they can't fire on us!" Nikolai said. "If they miss they could kill hundreds of innocent civilians!"

Lexi raised a cynical eyebrow. "And your point is what, exactly?"

"Lexi's right," Zeke said. "Remember, Faulkner was happy to set off that nuke and take out the whole city! No way he's going to think twice about giving these guys carte blanche to take us out, no matter what the collateral damage may be!"

"Zeke's on the money," Alex said hurriedly, her head hanging out the window once again and hair whipping in the wind. "We have an incoming missile at six o'clock, Joe!"

"I'm on it."

Hawke pulled the cyclic and tipped the chopper into a sharp right bank onto a busy Market Street, packed with gridlocked traffic. The Apache's Hellfire missile streaked across the junction behind them and ripped into the top floors of the Chase Bank building and blasted them to pieces. In the pursuant fireball, great chunks of masonry rained down onto Geary Street just behind the building, with a large piece of balcony crunching into the roof of an empty cab parked up below at the side of the street. The siren sounded and its lights began flashing. People screamed and ran for cover. Chaos had officially arrived in downtown San Francisco.

Hawke was already leaving it in his wake, skilfully navigating the Little Bird to the left and flying low over the top of the Ginto Japanese restaurant. He powered up and weaved the tiny chopper through the gap between the McKesson Corp building and the Citibank skyscraper. Montgomery Tower loomed ahead of them, seconds away. A full impact was unthinkable. He reacted fast, twisting the cyclic to the right and raising the collective, zipping the chopper out over Post Street and leaving a low building with an impressive rooftop garden in their wake turbulence. The engine whined and howled as he pushed it to the limit, but the chase was far from over.

"Another missile, Joe!" Alex screamed.

The Hellfire screeched past them, missing only when Hawke suddenly jerked the chopper down and to the right. When it blasted into the Hunter-Dulin building and ripped the top story to pieces, they all felt the shockwave. With masonry raining down in a giant, smoky fireball behind them, Hawke now pushed the chopper almost to street level. Barely skimming over the roofs of the cars trundling along Montgomery Street, he started to get the feeling they were running out of road in a big way.

And ideas.

"We need something more than just running, Alex."

"I'm on it."

He raced the chopper over California Street, deftly keeping the aircraft low and level as more skyscrapers flashed past them on either side. One slip at this speed and altitude would be instantly fatal; there would be no time to correct any kind of piloting error.

Zeke was now hanging out of the window in the back now, letting off a few rounds at the nearest Apache. It was a long shot, they all knew, including him, but if he was going to go, he was going to go out swinging. As the chopper raced past the famous Transamerica Pyramid building, he got lucky and struck something in the radar dome on top of the Apache. It exploded in a small fireball and then the gunship started to pull down to the ground.

"Got the bastard!" he yelled, sharing a high-five with Nikolai. Beside him, the green-faced monk was holding his stomach and trying not to throw up inside the chopper.

Up front, Hawke tipped his head out of his window, then came back inside. “You must have somehow damaged the rotor mast. Good work, Zeke.”

The Apache rammed into the junction at Montgomery and Washington and exploded in a colossal fireball. Hitting the ground at such high speed, it scraped and tumbled over the junction and skidded several hundred yards down Columbus Avenue. On its way, it took out a number of cars and pedestrians before its wreckage came to a bent, burning stop in the middle of the road.

“One down and two to go!” Zeke said.

“I don’t think the others are going to let that happen again, Tex,” Lexi said.

Hawke pushed the helicopter harder now, descending once again until he almost had to weave in and out of the traffic driving through Russian Hill. The two Apaches behind him fired together, each releasing a Hellfire missile at the same time. The two missiles screeched through the air and ripped either side of the Little Bird. Alex screamed again and even Lexi let a rare gasp of fear escape from her lips.

“They’re insane!” Zeke said. “Those missiles could land anywhere!”

“Not anywhere,” Hawke said. “There!”

He turned the chopper hard to the left just as the two missile ripped into Fisherman’s Wharf. One of them blew up a burger takeout restaurant and the other slammed in the famous Pier 39 where tourists gathered by day in their thousands to see Californian sea lions. Tonight, the entire pier went up in a firestorm, blasting upturned boats and obliterating fish restaurants and the aquarium into millions of pieces all over the smoking debris-strewn water.

As Hawke continued his hard bank to the left, Alex gripped her seat. “These guys are psychos, Joe!”

"Yeah, I'm just starting to get that."

"You got a plan to take out the other two?" Lexi said.

"I'm going to stick with my 'make it up as I go along' method, Lex," he said, bringing the Little Bird level and heading west toward the Golden Gate Bridge. "If that's all right with you."

She sighed. "You got me this far, I guess."

"Thanks, Hun."

"Wait," Zeke said, pointing at the world-famous bridge. "Does this 'making it up as we go along' thing involve that bridge?"

"I think it just might," Hawke said with a grin. "After all, it seems a shame to waste it."

Zeke shook his head as the marine district flashed beneath them. "You're one in a million, Hawke."

"That could be a good thing, or a bad thing," Alex said, craning her neck out of the window to see where the Apaches were.

"I'll take it as a good thing," Hawke said. "See anything?"

"I sure do," she said. "One of them has gone high again and the other is moving out wide to our right. He's turning! He's right on our doorstep, Joe!

Hawke turned and saw the second Apache heading out over the water. When it was parallel with Alcatraz Island, it turned abruptly to face them and unleashed another Hellfire missile. There was no time for commentary. Hawke pushed the cyclic forward and lowered the collective, sending the chopper down to the water, flying so low he almost hit the masts of the boats in the St. Francis Yacht Club. The missile was heading straight for them, cutting through the air like a razor and racing toward their starboard side. "It's going to hit us, Joe!" Alex screamed.

Everyone on board closed their eyes and prayed.

Everyone except Joe Hawke.

CHAPTER TWENTY-EIGHT

"Probably the Bushmaster chain guns," Brooke stared at the warship approaching them fast across the surface of Lake Michigan. "That bastard has two of them on deck. They're not nice. Thirty mil, even worse than the Apache's chain gun."

"Chain-gun time again," Lea said grimly. "Oh, happy day."

Then, several gondolas at the top of the Ferris Wheel exploded into thousands of pieces as the rounds from the warship's chain-gun ripped into them in a firestorm. Glass rained down all over the control room as the vessel flashed across the east tip of the pier and made a turn on its south side. Arcing around in the night like a sequence from some kind of nightmare, Lea watched the guns on its deck swivel around to aim at them once again.

"This can't be happening!" Kahlia said.

"We haven't got time for this!" said Lea.

Tawan's voice over the comms was calm and soft. "Nature does not hurry yet everything is accomplished."

Lea cursed in the control room. "Damn it Tawan! What the hell does that mean?"

"A Lao Tzu quotation," he said. "It means focus on your work in the gondola and we will deal with the warship."

Reaper shrugged. "Sounds like the best idea we have."

"Then get to it!"

The big Frenchman began the task of breaking off the weapon's steel casing and examining the interior contents. Wires, wires and more wires, and then he saw it

– rigged with a boobytrap. He kept it to himself – no point alarming the others and they didn't have time for it anyway. He wondered how Hawke and Scarlet's teams were doing in San Francisco and New York. As far as he knew, both the other cities were still standing, so maybe his old friends were doing all right.

He heard screaming and looked up from his work to see Brooke, Tawan and Kahlia sprinting down the pier. Tawan was pushing the hotdog cart and Brooke and Kahlia were on his flanks, arms raised with guns in the aim.

"What the hell are they doing?' he asked.

"They're saving our arses and buying us some time," said Lea. "They're making it look like they have the bomb in the cart and they're trying to take it off the pier."

The warship's guns swivelled and opened fire on Brooke's small team. Lea watched in horror as the massive rounds chewed into the pier, blasting it to pieces behind her friends as they ran for their lives. All just to buy them a few more minutes. A deep thump shook them in the control room and Lea watched a missile tearing away from the ship at the head of a twisting column of smoke.

"Holy crap," Lea said. "Jack! They're firing more than the chain gun at you!"

"We know!"

The explosion was terrific. A heavy, metallic bass roar as the warship now upped the ante and opened fire on them with one of their land-attack Naval Strike Missiles. It crashed into the middle of the pier just a few dozen yards behind Brooke and his team and then exploded, sending a massive fireball into the air and spraying thousands of pieces of the pier's now obliterated central section all over the lake.

"Are you okay?" Lea said, waiting patiently for a response.

Then, one of the warship's two MQ-8 Fire Scout unmanned autonomous helicopters took off from the deck and descended down to just a few feet above the water, flying in their direction.

"Jack?" she repeated. "Damn it! Jack?"

Static.

She turned to Reaper. "Update?"

"Nearly, but it's tricky work. I expect a raise when we get back to Elysium. It doesn't have to be money. Cigarettes and alcohol works just fine."

She searched for a smile but there were none left inside her to find. "Jack?"

"Yeah, we're good," he finally called back. "Sorry for the delay but Kahlia got knocked over in the blast so we had to stop to help her. She's fine. We're almost at the shore. Listen, that little bastard that just took off from the ship is dangerous. They're armed with Viper Strike laser-guided glide bombs. Judging by its speed and direction, I'd say our little ploy has been uncovered. Looks like it's heading your way. You have to get that damned bomb deactivated and get the hell out of there, Lea!"

She looked frantically at Reaper, who was now waving a black steel cylinder at her. "I have it."

"Already done," she called back. "And we have the trigger, too."

"Then let's get out of here," Brooke replied.

Lea and Reaper sprinted from the control room and aimed for the shore. With the entire central section of the pier now missing and Jack and his team on the other side, they both knew what they had to do. Lea jumped into the sea first, then Reaper snatched up a second pistol from one of the dead agents on the pier and now leaped into the sea behind her. As he fell through the air he twisted and raised both guns into the aim, blasting the drone out of the sky with a savage fusillade of gunfire.

They both fell from the sky together, crashing into the water at the same time. When he came to the surface, Lea was already treading water.

"What took you so long?"

"That's no way to talk to an old man."

She shrugged. "Last one back to the shore is buying the drinks."

*

With Kamala dead on the Stock Exchange's trading room floor, Scarlet fought hard to keep the rage down. The two women were good friends, but out in the field like this, she was Kamala's commanding officer and every CO knew the horror of losing someone under their command. Worse, her death had not been quick or painless. She had been shot and wounded and allowed to bleed for some time before finally being peppered with rounds from compact machine pistols. Now, her bullet-riddled corpse, soaked in blood, was sprawled out on the floor for all to see.

The ghost of Jack Camacho rose in Scarlet's tortured mind. Another of her teammates killed in action, only he was much more than that. He was her lover and her closest friend. She fought harder to keep the anger caged somewhere deep inside her, but this was a battle she was never going to win. She had repressed the death of Camacho in the way she had always done, the way she had buried the feelings she felt about watching her parents die when she was a small girl.

It worked most of the time, but now something snapped deep inside her.

Kamala.

Jack.

Her mother and her father.

The explosion inside her head and heart and soul was worse than any grenade or bomb detonation she had ever witnessed and now she reached into her pack and grabbed the modified carbine she had taken back in Tartarus from one of the dead airmen. Then, she broke cover.

Scarlet Sloane was going on a killing spree.

She would take her rage out on the enemy in here tonight and kill every single one of them or she would die trying. She charged them, firing a long burst of rounds from the GAU-5A as she ran alongside the others across the trading floor. The modified M4 carbine was a neat piece of kit designed by the USAF to break down into two pieces to enable storage inside aircraft ejector seats. Developed with an eye to giving downed pilots something to defend themselves with, tonight its use was entirely offensive. She raked the agents and the men in black Special Ops fatigues and gas masks one more time, sending them diving for cover. They crashed behind one of the large islands filled with trading screens, by day all flickering neon and new information, tonight, quiet and dark.

As her remaining team made the cover of another one of the islands, one of the Special Ops soldiers leaned around the corner of the screen and fired a long burst at her. Rounds nipped at her heels as she sprinted, pinging off in all directions and she pounded across the floor toward some cover. The last few rounds struck the famous bell up on the marble balcony above the Big Board's main trading floor. She didn't hang around to watch the ricochet, but dived to the floor behind the nearest desk and reloaded the carbine with her last magazine.

By day, this place was dominated by countless floor brokers buying and selling their clients' trades. Once a much noisier place, today many brokers sent their order flows out on computers anonymously. Tonight the noise was different – automatic weapons' fire and men screaming in pain and agony as Scarlet Sloane broke cover and charged on the enemy once more, mercilessly ripped them to pieces one by one until every last man and woman was nothing more than a dead heap covered in bloody rags.

"Christ, Cairo!" Ryan said, crawling out of his cover position. "That was brutal."

"That was for Kamala," she said, throwing the gun to the floor in disgust.

"A massacre," Ravi said in horror, making the sign of the cross over his face and chest.

Silence filled the seconds. "It's over," Scarlet said bluntly, loading a cigarette onto her lower lip and sparking it up with her lighter. "Now we take Faulkner out."

CHAPTER TWENTY-NINE

High over the Golden Gate strait, Alex screamed again as the missile sped toward them but Hawke yanked back on the controls and pulled the chopper into a steep climb way beyond the aircraft's flight envelope. The missile streaked beneath them, inches from their skids, speeded over the top of the Marina Airfield and ploughed into a number of residential homes in the Marina District, blasting them into a million pieces in a gigantic fireball that rose up into the air over the water. Thick black smoke bubbled out of the fireball and plumed up into the air above the totally destroyed homes.

"Holy crap," Zeke said. "We have to stop this!"

Sirens screamed down on Fillmore Street as emergency vehicles responded to the carnage back on Fisherman's Wharf. Now, some of them turned left on Marina Boulevard and diverted to the annihilated houses by the Palace of Fine Arts instead.

Hawke had taken as much of this as he could handle. The Apache was a formidable airborne killing machine but it had its weaknesses. He knew several of them had been shot down by rogue fighters in Iraq , and mostly this was done by getting closer and firing on the crew. In Iraq, they did this by hitting the gunships with a grenade attack and then taking the crews out with snipers. That wasn't an option tonight because they had no grenade launchers, but Zeke had already demonstrated his ability to take out one of the choppers. Maybe he could work his Texan magic again.

"Zeke, the only way we get this thing off our arse is if you can take out the driver. Can you do it?"

The Texan held onto a grab handle as Hawke turned the chopper violently to the right again to avoid incoming fire from the second Apache's chain gun.

"I sure can, Joe. Just get me close enough."

"Consider it done, and hang on everyone. This is going to take some of the roughest flying any of you have ever enjoyed."

"Enjoyed?" Alex said, tightening her belt. "Are you sick?"

"Yes. Yes, I think I am," Hawke said with a grin. "Now hold on!"

He banked the chopper so hard to the right that they were almost flying on their side. Alex stared down and saw the surface of the bay sparkling in the early moonlight but felt like she was about to throw up. He started to lose lift, but corrected the attitude and straightened up until he was facing the Apache.

"I heard of playing chicken," Zeke said, readying his gun, "but this is insane."

The Apache raced toward them, firing the chain gun and releasing another Hellfire missile.

Hawke held his nerve, pulling the chopper up at the last minute and allowing the machinegun rounds to trace either side of the Little Bird. The missile roared underneath them, shaking the chopper in its wake. The rounds went into the night but the missile scorched its way at the head of a trail of smoke over a picnic area and into the famous open rotunda of the Palace of Fine Arts. Masonry and soil and water from the lake blew up all over the place in another grotesque assault on the city as the Apache was about to flash past them.

"Now, Zeke!" Hawke yelled.

The Texan was already hanging out of his window and now he opened fire. Emptying an entire new magazine at the windows of the Apache as it raced alongside them, he buried at least three rounds into the windshield and took out the two crew members in a shocking display of marksmanship.

"Holy shit," Lexi said. "You did it!"

As Zeke pulled back inside the Little Bird, the Apache was already hundreds of yards behind them. Hawke turned the chopper and they all watched the gunship drop down into the bay and explode on the surface in a massive splash. Bent rotors and a twisted tail boom were the first things they saw as the giant spray of water settled down around the wreck. Then, the entire aircraft began to sink beneath the waves.

"Good work, Zeke," Alex said. "That just leaves number three."

"But they're not exactly going to fall for the same trick a third time, are they?" Lexi said.

"No," Hawke said flatly.

"So what are we going to do then?" she asked.

He turned and grinned. "Have you already forgotten about the bridge?"

No one had any time to talk. With the final Apache now descending and pulling in behind them, the ex-SBS man was already driving the helicopter hard toward the bridge's southern tower. Descending until low enough to fly under it, he banked hard to the right and flew the Little Bird directly beneath the six lane highway above.

"Never done this before!" he said cheerily.

"Focus, Joe," Alex said.

Hawke laughed as he raced the chopper underneath the old, nineteen-thirties art deco span bridge. "I'm always focussed. It's my main character flaw."

She rolled her eyes. "What would I do without you?"

"Probably live a life of peaceful contemplation," he said, turning the chopper once again into a hard starboard bank and flying sharply around the southern tower. Increasing speed, he brought the helicopter up at a steep angle and flew over the top of the bridge. Levelling it off, he was now flying at speed over the top of the cars driving north into Marin County.

Behind them, the Apache closed the gap but flew too close to the massive suspender cables and just nipped them with the edges of its rotors before whipping violently around in a tight arc, propelled back into the cables by the rotating motion of the blades.

Hawke watched as the Apache's rotors smashed once again into the massive suspender cables. Sparks exploded in the night as the pilot struggled to control the gunship but it was already too late and now it plummeted to the highway below like a dead bird. It screeched through the air with a howling roar and trailing a twisting column of black smoke behind it as it fell back to earth. Mercifully, when it crashed into the highway it narrowly missed a flatbed truck transporting some agricultural equipment on the northward lanes. Then, a fuel leak ignited and the entire aircraft disappeared in a massive fireball.

Hawke was prepared for the shockwave and took evasive action to keep the Little Bird level when it hit them. Then, finally, the night fell silent.

Alex was first to speak. "How did you know that was going to happen?"

Hawke grinned. "Whatever are you talking about?"

She sighed. "C'mon, Hawke. You know what I'm talking about. How could you know that was going to happen to them?"

He shrugged. "How did I know they would clip their wings?"

"Uh-huh."

He grinned. "Little Bird rotor diameter is six meters shorter than Apache rotor diameter. Gotta know your specs before you go to war, Reeve."

She smiled and squeezed his arm. "Thanks for saving me, again."

"Don't mention it." Hawke rotated away from the devastation and flew them away into the darkness above the bridge. "Now, we put this thing down and get our heads together."

Moments later they landed on the cliffs on the western side of Marin County. Still in shock, no one spoke for a long time. Then, with the rotors spinning to a stop behind him, Hawke wandered away from the chopper to make the call to the other teams. Zeke watched the bloody, bruised English marine pacing up and down along the cliff as he spoke into the cell phone, his body lit silver by a moon rising over San Francisco Bay behind them. When he slipped the phone into his pocket and walked back over to them, his face had changed. It was still strong and determined, but a light had gone out.

"What's the matter, Joe?" Alex asked.

"That was Cairo."

"They stopped the bomb, right?" she asked nervously.

He nodded. "Yeah, they stopped the bomb. They have the trigger, just like us and Lea's team, too."

"So why do you look like that?" Lexi asked.

"Because we lost Kamala. She was killed by men working for Faulkner inside the Stock Exchange."

"My God…" Alex said quietly. "Poor Kamala."

Hawke pushed his hands in his pockets and turned to face the ocean. Far below, on the cliffs enveloping Tennessee Valley Beach, the waves crashed onto the shore with a harsh, angry roar that seemed to reflect how they all felt about their friend's death. "Apparently, she died saving Ravi's life."

“God, he must feel awful,” Alex said.

“Not as awful as Davis Faulkner is about to feel,” Hawke said quietly. “C’mon, we’re meeting everyone in New York before we go down to DC. Let’s end this nightmare.”

CHAPTER THIRTY

Josh Muston hesitated at the northeast door of the Oval Office and rehearsed one more time exactly what he was ging to tell the president. Behind him, the president's private secretary was tapping away at the computer on her desk, and a young man in a suit was quietly cursing and fighting with an argumentative coffee machine. The atmosphere was relaxed and calm, but it wouldn't be for long. That was why he was hesitating and thinking things through. The best way to break the news, and save his career.

Knock knock knock.

"Enter."

Muston pushed open the door and stepped inside the world's most famous office. Now, after so long working here every day, it had become ordinary, almost banal. Smaller than he thought it would be, too. What wasn't ordinary and banal was the look on the face of the man smoking a cigar behind the desk at the other end of the room.

"This had better be good news, Josh."

"No, sir. I'm afraid it is not."

Faulkner fixed him with a death glare and sat up straighter in his chair. "Out with it."

"Operation Perses is over, Mr President."

"What the hell are you talking about?"

"It's ECHO, sir. They broke into sub-units and attacked the three ground zero sites simultaneously. The mini-nukes in San Francisco, Chicago and New York are all neutralized. Backup teams sent into each site confirm the neutron triggers for each weapon have been successfully removed after deactivation protocols were initiated."

Faulkner paled and slumped back down into his seat. "I don't understand. How did this happen? Those bombs are central to our plan. They're how we frame ECHO and Brooke once and for all and shift public opinion into accepting my third term as president. Without those, public opinion will never shift the way we need it to on my continued leadership."

"They're gone, sir. Deactivated and damaged beyond repair by the ECHO team."

Faulkner jumped from his chair, his face suddenly red with rage. With the swivel chair still spinning around behind him, he slammed his fist down on the desk, smashed his telephone onto the floor and roared in a display of unbridled anger Muston had never before witnessed. "This is totally unacceptable, Josh! You were charged with the grave responsibility of ensuring the protection of those weapons and my goddam presidency! Now the bombs are gone and… wait a minute. Where are ECHO right now?"

The obvious second question, Muston thought. "We have no exact location at this time, sir, but we believe they'll be heading to Washington DC as fast as they can move. Brooke is with them and it's likely they will try and take back the White House."

Faulkner laughed, but nervously. "They can't just come in here and *take back the White House*, Josh! I'm the president, legally. Approved by the cabinet via the Twenty-Fifth Amendment due to Brooke's treasonous behavior. They can't just come in here and demand I resign! And even if I do, then the office passes to the Vice President, not Brooke. What else are they going to do, kill me?"

Muston paused in the tense office a second too long. Long enough for the penny to drop.

"You can't be serious?" Faulkner said. "They can't kill me! That's assassination of a sitting president! They'll go to Gitmo for fifty years and then get sent to the chair!"

"Right now, sir, we have no way of knowing what their plans are. But we're not helpless. We have the US Secret Service and we have the usual escape routes from the White House. They're not going to lay a hand on you. I swear it, Mr President."

Faulkner padded around the desk and squared up to him, jabbing his finger in his chest, cigar clamped in his teeth. "You had better be right, Muston. Remember what I told you when we spoke last? I go down, *you* go down. Got that?"

Muston nodded his head. "Whatever they're planning, they're all going to be dead within the next few hours."

"Pray you are right, boy," Faulkner snarled. "Or it's Krios."

Muston's mouth went dry. "If I pray for anything, sir, it's that Krios won't be necessary."

"It'll be goddam necessary if those bastards get anywhere near me or my presidency!"

"Yes, sir, Mr President." Muston took a step back, desperate to get to the door. Krios was the kind of nightmare no one in their right mind would ever want to experience. "And with that in mind, sir, it's time to make sure we're ready for the final showdown with ECHO."

"Good, get on it now or as I say, it's Krios."

Muston hurried from the room, his mind frozen by the fear of just one simple word.

Krios.

"Perfectly put, Tawan," said Alex.

Lexi and Scarlet rolled their eyes. "Still boring," Scarlet said.

"And let's be honest," Lexi said. "Faulkner is not going down without one hell of a fight. I would be surprised if he doesn't kill himself rather than be taken prisoner by us and put on trial. That is exactly what he was planning to do to you, Jack. Can you imagine all the fantasies he's had on that subject? Now he sees the tables being turned and he's not going to like it. It's going to terrify him. My money's on suicide before we get to him."

"A luger-in-the-library job is entirely possible," Ryan mused.

"Either way, we're not killing him unless it's in self-defence," Brooke said firmly. "Anyone who can't handle that should not be on this team. At least, not if their objective is to help me get back into the White House. I can't sit behind that desk with the previous president's blood on my hands, no matter how he got there. It's not ethical and it's not politically expedient, either. If he dies, it must be in self-defense."

"Then that's decided," Hawke said. "We proceed with care and only take out people who present an immediate threat to our lives, up to and including Josh Muston and Davis Faulkner. After that, things get messier politically, but that's a problem for you, Jack. We're not a political force and we won't get involved."

"I understand."

"But on that subject," Lea asked. "Is there a way you can legally get back into power?"

Brooke didn't have to consider her question. He had been thinking about nothing else since the day of his arrest. "Yes, I think so. If it can be shown that Faulkner enacted the Twenty-Fifth Amendment on false pretences, and of course it *can* be shown, then there is a strong argument the whole process was unlawful and in fact constituted a coup."

Alex raised her hand, sheepishly. "And there's something else, too."

Everyone turned to stare at her, but it was Jack Brooke who broke the silence. "What is it, darling?"

"You know how Ryan and I spent most of the flight from Tartarus to the US on his laptop?"

"Uh-huh."

"We worked some white hat hacking magic on some of the members of Faulkner's new cabinet. Just looked into their pasts a little. We found connections with radical political groups in Russia and China, dirty money in the way of bribes, payments from corrupt oligarchs for services unknown, and some personal material I can't bring myself to talk about out loud."

"I will!" Ryan said.

"No, you won't," she said, turning and staring at him. Her frown turned to a smile, and everyone on board saw a spark between them. She broke her gaze away and turned back to the team. "The point is, we can send this information out to these people and demand they resign from the cabinet."

"That's blackmail," Brooke said.

"They shouldn't be in the cabinet, Dad. You know it, and I know it."

"We all know it," Hawke said firmly. "And I don't want to know what any of them have been getting up to, but if we can use it to get them out, then I say we do it."

"Agreed," Lea said.

"Count me in," said Scarlet. "I'm voting for it just for Kamala. I'd do anything to the bastards behind this war on us… behind the death of so many of our friends."

Everyone else nodded.

"Okay," Brooke said with a weary sigh. He turned to Alex. "I'll need to see what you have, first. If I agree to it, then send it out and let's hope and pray we get the mass resignations. If we've already taken Faulkner out of the game by that point, we would essentially have no executive branch of government."

"There won't be any problem with Faulkner," Ryan said, spinning his laptop around. "What we have here is an email trail between him and various members of his new cabinet, before the coup, in which they discuss framing you for a number of crimes. He's as guilty as a feather-covered fox in a henhouse."

"That's sedition," Brooke said. "If it's true."

"It's true, and you'll know when you read it."

"The email addresses could have been faked."

"Sure, but not the Zoom call I found between Faulkner and Josh Muston talking about setting up the whole thing. It's over."

Brooke breathed out a sigh of relief. "My God, if that's true then just maybe we can do this. If we can show Faulkner planned this, the Twenty-Fifth Amendment he used to force me from power would be null and void. I would still be the president – right now and since the moment he invoked it."

"Maybe we should just leak it on the internet and save ourselves the bother fighting," Zeke said.

Alex and Ryan both went to speak at the same time, and laughed. Another little shared moment, Lea thought. Alex said, "That wouldn't work. These guys can control the entire internet. They decide who sees what and when. Worse, Faulkner controls the entire press. Even if it leaks, they'll ban it from everywhere and call it a deep fake, relegate it to the darkest corners of the internet and brand anyone who supports it a conspiracy theorist."

"Alex is right," Hawke said. "Faulkner is a man of power and violence and greed. Only violence can bring him down. The fate of the world is now in our hands. Only we can do what needs to be done tonight, and it might be that not all of us are going to make it. We've already lost Kamala in the last few hours. There could be more loss."

A long tense, silence as they looked around the cockpit at each other, everyone wondering if Hawke was right. Wondering who might not be coming home after the battle.

"So what happens next?" Ryan said, finally breaking the silence.

Brooke said, "Once I've seen the material Alex and you put together, and if I agree we can use it, I'll spend the rest of the flight down to DC calling trusted colleagues from across government who I can ask into the cabinet. This plus the dirt you and Alex dug up on Faulkner and the rest of those bastards puts Faulkner in a ton of shit and me back behind the Resolute Desk. That's the path I'm going to use, anyway."

"And it's going to work," Alex said. "It *has* to work. You barely got started with your domestic reforms and foreign policy initiatives before that maniac threw us in prison. Now you have to go and undo all the crazy stuff he's been doing since coming to power and push on with your agenda – the one the people voted for in such large numbers."

Brooke smiled, proud of his daughter's loyalty and support. Still grinning, he said, "I love you, darling, but I can't make you Chief-of-Staff, no matter how much you support me. They'd cry nepotism and they'd be right."

She laughed. "That's one job I really do *not* want!"

After a moment of humor, the mood darkened when the team remembered the gravity of the situation facing them. It was, they knew, the most dangerous moment

ECHO had ever faced, and failure meant death for each one of them. Worse, none of them knew if they would all make it home again. The battle for the White House was not one Davis Faulkner and his forces would wage lightly.

Breaking the gloomy tension, Hawke turned in his seat and glanced at the instruments one more time. “All right, everyone – we’re landing in fifteen minutes.”

Lea watched out of the window as the plane descended through the clouds and an ocean of lights appeared below. Hawke banked the plane and lined up with College Park Airport, just over the Maryland border from DC. She heard the whine of hydraulics as Hawke extended the flaps and lowered the undercarriage, locking it into position.

Something told her she was about to find herself deep in the toughest fight of her life.

And the history of the world turned on the outcome.

CHAPTER THIRTY-TWO

Marching through the streets of Washington DC, Jack Brooke experienced a sensation he had first felt back in Chicago, but this time it was even weirder. All serving presidents and former presidents never went anywhere without a US Secret Service detail, all around them, fully armed and linked to heavy duty backup with comms. Didn't matter if that was a flight to another city or a walk to the local Starbucks. They went nowhere without the detail. Tonight, moving through the streets of the nation's capital with his daughter and ECHO just felt plain *wrong*.

The feeling was compounded when they turned the corner of Pennsylvania Avenue and saw the White House illuminated in floodlights up ahead of them. On the outside looking in, he thought, was not a great feeling, especially when you stopped to think about who was actually inside the place, sitting beside the Resolute Desk, slowly stripping Americans of their hard-won liberties and freedoms. That thought sent a chill up his spine but the determination on the faces of his friends at his sides returned his courage to him. Tonight they would see justice, he knew it in his heart.

He turned to his right and saw Alex walking beside him. He felt mixed emotions. Seeing her back on her feet, picking up the pace at his side was the best feeling in the world, but two things blackened his joy. First, could the elixir be relied upon? He worried about it failing at a critical moment in the battle, leaving his daughter vulnerable to attack. Second, they were not walking to the local park for an ice cream, but toward the fight of their lives. She was out of shape, unused to so much physical activity.

She always asked him to trust her judgement, but tonight that was harder than ever. Then, his thoughts were interrupted by Lea Donovan. She was nudging him and pointing with her other arm along the dark sidewalk.

"Is that the old friend you told us about after the calls you made on the plane?"

Jack Brooke peered into the darkness. He stared for a while, calculating the figure walking toward him – body mass, height, gait, walking speed. Then, a smile appeared on his face. "Yeah, that's him."

Hawke reached inside his jacket and gripped his gun just in case, but it was unnecessary.

The president and the other man gave each other a hearty handshake and a brief, soldierly pat on the back. Then Brooke turned to his friends with a broad smile. "I'd like to introduce you to General Mike Mulkey."

"Good evening, General," Lea said. "I'd ask how you are, but I think we all feel the same tonight."

Mulkey gave a cautious laugh. "I think we can agree on that."

Brooke said, "I've known Mike for over thirty years. He's a highly decorated veteran and has a distinguished service record. Not only that, but he makes a mean barbecue. I trust him with my life."

"I don't even trust *me* with my life," Mulkey joked, but the smile faded fast. Everyone knew Brooke didn't say things like this lightly.

"Mike's going to help us get the White House back tonight, right?" said Brooke.

"With the help of some of my most trusted friends," he said. "We sure are. Is everything we spoke about when you were on the plane in place?"

Brooke nodded. "Sure is. The intel Alex and Ryan got was all good and genuine. They emailed most of Faulkner's cabinet and told them to resign or they'd email it to their loved ones and whatever press would carry it. Then I spoke to a number of trusted colleagues from various government departments. They all agreed to join the new cabinet I'll be forming tonight after Davis Faulkner steps down from the presidency."

"And you're sure he'll do that?"

"One way or the other, Mike, he'll be going tonight."

"That's enough for me, Mr President. Let's go. Follow me, please."

"But the White House is this way," Lexi said.

"We're not going to the White House," Mulkey said. "Are we, Jack?"

"I guess not," Brooke said. "But I think I know where we *are* going."

*

"Way back in 1861," Mulkey began, "a man named General Winfield Scott…"

"Also known as Old Fuss and Feathers because of his strict adherence to military uniform and code," Brooke said with a smile.

"That's the guy," Mulkey continued. "Anyway, General Scott started to have grave concerns about a confederate attack on Washington during the Civil War. This was right after the Battle of Fort Sumter in the April of that year, down near Charleston. He had the brilliant idea of the president retreating to the much chunkier and more easily defended Treasury Building running along 15th Street NW, just off to the east of the White House."

"Sounds like a smart man," Lea said.

"He was," Mulkey said. "And I say that as a Texan. Anyway, he had the Treasury Building's defenses increased, including stationing more soldiers around it and barricading interior doors. The idea was that if the city was overrun by the enemy, soldiers defending the White House would delay them there while Abraham Lincoln retreated to the vaults inside the Treasury. It was a dangerous and uncertain time."

"Not dissimilar from tonight, darling," Scarlet said.

"So they built a tunnel from the White House to the Treasury?" Lea asked.

"No, the tunnel didn't happen until much later, after the attack on Pearl Harbor in 1941. After that, there were even greater concerns about the president's safety, especially from air attack. So they constructed a specially reinforced bunker beneath the White House's East Wing to shield him from attack. Problem was that took time, so they came up with a temporary measure."

"The Treasury Building?"

"Right," Mulkey said. "They built a presidential suite consisting of ten rooms directly below the vaults in the Treasury Building, protected behind steel doors. Then they excavated a tunnel from the East Wing over to the Treasury Building to get the president there without him having to break cover and use the road."

"And it's still there?" Scarlet asked.

"It sure is," Brooke said. "Presidents use it all the time, and so do their guests and families. LBJ used it to avoid people protesting against the Vietnam War, for one. And I'm about to use it tonight, but in the opposite direction as usual. Right, Mike?"

Mulkey pulled out his security clearance. "Yes, Mr President, you sure are."

"You think you can get us in the tunnel with that clearance, Mike?" Brooke asked.

"I know I can. Both the men guarding the tunnel are loyal to me, sir. After that, things are going to get harder. As arranged earlier, once you're inside the tunnel, I'll head back to my office and organize air support in case things get out of control. We'll be in contact the entire time."

Brooke patted him on the shoulder. "In that case, we'd better get to it, General."

CHAPTER THIRTY-THREE

Hawke was beside Brooke and Lea as they marched down the subterranean tunnel. Faces like hardened steel, they had no way of knowing what they were walking into, but they knew they had to do it. Behind them, the rest of the ECHO team, including the three new members they seemed to have picked up on Tartarus, dutifully followed, guns in hand.

The tunnel was mostly bare concrete with some sections painted white. Emergency lighting was fixed to the wall in case of a fire and the whole place was damp and had a strange unused feeling. Kahlia shuddered as they made their way down it. She had never been afraid of anything back in Hawaii. A tough childhood and even tougher teenage years had carved a strong, unyielding young woman who gave no quarter, but her life had changed so fast in the last few years she hardly knew what to think.

Except she wasn't on Ehukai Beach anymore, *Toto*.

She was marching through a tunnel under the nation's capital on her way to storm the White House with the former President of the United States at her side. Ravi was still with her, thank God. Not that she would tell him, but she wouldn't be able to this without him. I mean, who the hell *are* these people? An English commando dude with a death wish, a battle-hardened Irishwoman, a guy from the French Foreign Legion, a Chinese assassin… C'mon, man. This isn't real.

But when the lights went out, she knew it was real.

"All right. Torches on and guns out, everyone," Hawke said. "They know we're here."

Deep under the streets of Washington's second ward, the darkness was total and the only sound was their footfall and breathing. Kahlia shone her flashlight along the tunnel and felt another shiver go up her spine. Then, as they approached the far end of the corridor, a big set of steel double doors up ahead of them burst open and muzzle flash strobed like a wild electrical storm.

"Down!" Hawke yelled.

The team crashed to the floor as Hawke fired back. Reaper and Scarlet joined him, peppering the men up ahead with a lethal barrage of fire. Bullets sprayed everywhere, but the team was protected by their powerful Maglite beams blinding the attackers night vision goggles. As their rounds ripped through the bodies of the men defending the White House, screams echoed coldly and blood sprayed up the white plaster walls. Dead men collapsed onto the concrete floor and the few who had survived ECHO's spirited defense turned and fled behind the steel doors.

"Forward!" Hawke yelled.

Kahlia felt that shiver again, but before she knew it she was up on her feet with her gun in her hand and running alongside him.

"What's the punishment for breaking into the White House and trying to kill the president?" she called out, trying to calm her nerves with banter.

"It's treason," Ryan said. "So the penalty is death, probably after about twenty years on Death Row."

"We're not trying to kill Faulkner," Brooke said. "We need him alive. He has to face justice for what he has done to our Constitution."

"Talk later," Hawke said, clambering over the dead bodies. "Now we fight."

He kicked open the double doors and swung his gun in a defensive arc. The men who had fired on them were at the bottom of a set of wooden stairs, leading up to what Brooke had told them was the East Wing of the famous building above their heads. Behind them, others were scrambling down the steps, sidearms gripped in their hands.

Hawke led from the front, gun in hand as he charged toward the defensive line. The enemy was no pushover. These men and women were US Secret Service, some of the most highly trained professionals in the world, but he was an ex-Royal Marine Commando and Special Boat Service operative. He knew of no higher, or longer, or more demanding training on Earth and had the confidence that came with that knowledge.

He opened fire on them, instantly picking off three on the left. Their response was hot and fast, unleashing a barrage of rounds and sending ECHO diving for cover behind large concrete columns supporting the tunnel entrance at their backs. Hawke leaned around one of the columns and fired on the men again, desperate to stop them making it out alive.

Reaper understood it too, and tossed a grenade at the stairs. The explosion blew out the bottom five steps and sprayed wood and blood and limbs all over the basement. Shielded by the concrete stanchions, the ECHO team now poured more fuel on the fire and emptied their mags on the survivors. A minute of heavy gunfire established ECHO had the superiority and now the surviving agents fled up the stairs.

They broke cover, keen to get up into the main building before Faulkner was airlifted to safety. Alex ran as fast as her newly empowered legs could take her, supercharged by a buzz of wild excitement at the thought of finally clearing her father's name and getting Faulkner put in jail for his crimes. She edged ahead of Hawke on the stairs. Ryan was behind her as she turned on the landing to climb the remaining steps into the East Wing.

That was when it happened. A bloodied, soot-streaked Secret Service agent appeared above her head from behind a wooden banister rail and dropped a grenade right on top of her. She felt Ryan before she heard him. The young ECHO warrior slammed into her and bundled her to the ground with seconds to spare. The blast from the grenade ripped over the top of them both in a speeding firestorm as he shielded her from the heat and flames with his body, eyes clamped shut to save his sight.

Hers were shut too as she felt his weight pressing down on her. Then it was over, and he was rolling off. He leaped up and reached down to help her up. She reached out and he grabbed her, pulling her roughly to her feet. For the first time, she was seeing Ryan Bale in a very different way. For a few seconds, the annoying know-it-all nerd was gone and instead she saw a tough, battle-hardened young man, shaved head, sharp, determined eyes. Slightly sad smile. A man.

"You okay?" he said.

"I think so… thanks."

"No problem. We have to get moving if we're going to catch the others up."

"Yeah."

She followed him up the explosion-scorched stairs, knowing something had just happened but unsure exactly what. Was it possible she had feelings for Ryan? *Get yourself together, Reeve*, she thought. *Now is hardly the time for thinking like that.* But watching him pound along the corridor, assault rifle in his hand… maybe it wasn't such a crazy thought. He was about her age, highly intelligent, fit and lean and brave.

Yeah… *get yourself together, Reeve.*

She heard an explosion behind them. Another grenade had detonated, but mercifully this time they were too far away to be touched by its shockwave. Looking ahead over Ryan's shoulder she saw Reaper and Scarlet. They were standing at the top of the stairs, guns in their hands.

"Hurry!" the Frenchman called out.

"Good work, guys," said Scarlet. "I'm impressed, even by *you* boy."

"I'll take that as a serious compliment," Ryan said.

After what he had just done to save her life, Alex found herself wanting to defend him against Scarlet's constant insulting sniping, but she kept her mouth shut. Ryan and Scarlet had known each other before she came on the scene and they had their own special relationship. Besides, what business of it was hers?

Get yourself together, Reeve, right?

"How many more down there?" Reaper asked.

"Maybe half a dozen," Ryan said. "Hard to tell. What I can say with confidence is that they are in no way shy of using hand-thrown explosive weaponry. In fact, I would say they actively enjoy it."

"Put as only you could put it," Scarlet said.

As they walked past her, Scarlet and Reaper saw for the first time the scorch marks all over Ryan's back, including some tinged hair.

"Bloody hell, boy," Scarlet said. "What the hell happened?"

"He saved my life is what happened," Alex said. "He formed a human shield around me in the grenade blast, so maybe you should stop calling him boy and start calling him a man?"

Scarlet raised an eyebrow, accompanied by the briefest and most subtle of smirks. "Easy girl! Is there something I should know?"

Ryan turned and looked from Scarlet to Alex. "Eh?"

"Nothing at all," Alex said. "So let's get moving while we still can, all right? Dad still needs us, if you haven't already forgotten."

"I have *not* forgotten," Scarlet said. "And you're right. We *do* need to get going. Reaper and I will go ahead and you and your new wife can take the rear."

Alex scowled. "Enough, Cairo!"

Ryan was even more confused. "What the hell is going on here?"

"I think we all need to shut our mouths and move on," Reaper said. "Alex is right. The President of the United States is counting on us for everything right now. If he falls, America falls. If America falls, the rest of the Western world will be next."

"So, no pressure then," Scarlet said with a grin.

"Follow me, everyone," Brooke said from ahead of them. "We need to go through the Residence and then past the press briefing room into the West Wing. Faulkner always works late, so that's where he'll be at this time of night, plus they have the escape chute there in case of an emergency, which I'm guessing they're just working out is happening right now."

"Escape chute?" Ravi asked. "Is there such a thing?"

"Oh yeah," Brooke said. "Right under the president's desk."

"All right, then let's go," Lea said, then she checked the comms. "Everyone still reading me?"

Everyone checked in.

"Good. Then it's time to end this. Let's go get Faulkner."

CHAPTER THIRTY-FOUR

Lea Donovan charged along the unlit West Colonnade, gun in hand. She couldn't count the number of times she had seen a president walking along this famous path. White House staff called it the forty-five second commute because of the time it took the Commander-in-Chief to walk from his home in the Residence to his place of work.

The Oval Office.

She ran faster. The rose garden was on her left and the press briefing room on her right. She saw it through the windows, a place she had also seen a thousand times on the news. Some of the biggest breaking news in history had been broadcast to the world from this room. She had also seen it with her own eyes and the same went for the Oval Office, too.

"Started life as a swimming pool."

"Eh?" She turned to Ryan, jogging alongside her with a goofy grin on his face.

"The press office briefing room you were just looking at. President Franklin Roosevelt used to swim laps in it to help with his physio."

"Another fascinating fact delivered with impeccable timing," Scarlet said. "Thank you, Bale."

"More than welcome, Hun."

Ahead Lea saw the Oval Office, slightly to her left and getting closer by the second. She saw movement inside. Men in black suits rushing to the desk and talking to a man sitting behind it. Faulkner. Drapes were hurriedly closed. "We're running out of time. They're taking him!"

Hawke was adjacent to the door on the east side of the Oval Office. He lifted his gun and fired shots into the glass. They shattered it but got nowhere close to breaking it.

"That's gonna take a long time," Brooke said. "It's seriously bullet-proof."

"Then how?" Lea said.

"This way!"

They followed the president back along the north-south section of the colonnade, halfway back to the press room. Here, he raised his gun and fired into the glass, shattering a pane out of the window of one of the doors. Hawke bundled past him, lifting his leg and kicking it as hard as he could. Without the glass reinforcing the door, his riot boot easily smashed the thick wooden mullions out of the way and gave enough room to lean around and open the handle.

Door open and inside. The lights went down. Green emergency lighting gave an eerie glow as figures streamed out of a door to their left and started firing on them.

Hawke pushed Brooke back out of the door and opened fire one-handed on the men as he took cover behind the broken doorframe. Half a mag, then all the mag emptied on the men. Three of them fell down onto the carpet. One rolled all the way down a shallow carpeted access ramp built for wheelchairs.

"In!" Hawke yelled. "Everyone in! This is it!"

Up the slope and around the corner and he was standing outside the Cabinet Room. The large room was empty and they quickly made their way around the leather chairs positioned around a large conference table and out into the hall. Then, the Roosevelt Room. Fine, old oil paintings of Theodore Roosevelt who built the West Wing, and Franklin Roosevelt who renovated it, took pride of place. They also took the brunt of more firing as more US Secret Service agents took up a defensive position outside the door on the other side of the room and opened fire on who they believed were nothing more than rebels and insurgents.

Hawke returned fire, ripping chunks in the leather chairs and plaster walls and punching a line of bullet holes right across Teddy Roosevelt's face.

"That's gonna leave a mark," Scarlet shouted.

Brooke, on his stomach now alongside everyone else, took cover behind the heavy cabinet table and winced. "Yeah, that's gonna need some restoration."

"Sorry!" Hawke said.

ECHO fought valiantly, pushing forward, clearing the cabinet room and the corridor outside and then finally into the Oval Office. Hawke kicked open the northwest door just in time to see Muston screaming and Secret Service agents pushing Faulkner over towards the escape chute.

This was not the first time Hawke had been inside the Oval Office, but it was the first time in the dark and the first time he had gone in armed and fired rounds in it. With the gun still blazing in his hand, he threw himself into a rolling dive and landed behind one of the two long couches in the center of the room.

The Secret Service detail unleashed a brutal response, with one man emptying his magazine on him as the other hit the lever that opened the trap door behind the desk. It happened as fast as lightning. The guy operating the trapdoor now manhandled Faulkner roughly into the escape chute while the other continued to pour fire all over Hawke. Reaper and Scarlet were next in, opening fire on the agent and striking him multiple times in the chest. He fell backwards and died on the Resolute Desk but the other agent and Faulkner were long gone.

Muston was left standing to the side of the desk, looking like he was about to throw up.

"Freeze!" Hawke screamed. "Do not move!"

Faulkner and the Secret Service agents might be already gone, but the Chief of Staff was alive and kicking and right in front of him. As ECHO piled into the room behind Hawke, Muston now panicked and dived over the Resolute Desk. Hawke fired, punching spider-web fractures in the windows behind the desk and blasting Faulkner's private family photos to smithereens, but it was too late. Two suited trouser legs vanished from view down into the chute and by the time the Englishman had made it around the desk, the chute trap was shut and bolted.

Reaper ran to the northeast door and saw the president's secretary's office was empty. "Clear."

Scarlet moved like a shadow across the darkened office and checked the study and dining room to the west of the Oval Office. "Clear here, too."

"But not for long," Alex said.

"Alex is right," Brooke said. "We just attacked the White House with guns and tried to capture the sitting President. This place will probably have hundreds of marines all over it in seconds.

"Damn it all to hell!" Hawke yelled. "We weren't fast enough. He got away."

Brooke walked over to the desk, deep in thought. "Not necessarily."

"Care to expand?" Lea said.

"Yeah," Kahlia said, her intricate face tattoos looking even stranger in the moonlit office. "What makes you say that?"

Brooke grinned. "Because I know where they're taking Faulkner tonight."

CHAPTER THIRTY-FIVE

Camp David is the president's country retreat, situated deep in the forests of Maryland's Catoctin Mountain Park. By law, this rural presidential residence is a military installation formally referred to as the Naval Support Facility Thurmont and its tranquil isolation stretches over one hundred and forty acres of wooded hills. Every president since Franklin Delano Roosevelt back in 1942 has used the facility, often to use its eighteen-hundred foot elevation to escape the hot, humid summers of Washington DC.

None of this mattered one iota to Davis Faulkner as Marine One rotated ninety degrees above the facility's helipad and slowly descended toward the tree line. The president was rattled. Nervous and showing signs of cracking. This isn't how things were supposed to work out. He had an agenda to roll out, but instead he was turning tail and scuttling away to the hills like a frightened rabbit.

God damn ECHO, he thought. You get what you pay for, and right now he was seriously starting to regret hiring Josh Muston. He needed someone with an iron will at his side, not a goddam Georgetown pen-pushing lawyer. Hawke and ECHO should have been destroyed long ago, just like Brooke. All gone and out with the trash. Instead, they had regrouped and were threatening to take everything from him.

He looked outside the rumbling helicopter once again. The night was black, its cold darkness covering the world below. Here and there, he saw the various lights of buildings in the retreat as the Sikorsky VH-92A finally touched down. It looked peaceful, quiet, safe. But for how long?

Hawke and the rest of his bastard team had used insider knowledge and security clearances to gain entry to the White House. More names to heap on the ever-growing pile of traitors. Their invasion of the place seemed impossible enough to believe but it was as nothing compared to the bloody mayhem and havoc they had created there after getting in. The traitors who had assisted their ingress into the heart of the executive branch would pay dearly for their actions tonight, but Hawke and the others would face a much harsher punishment.

No more Most Wanted Lists. Eden, Hawke, Donovan. Brooke and his girl. Their days were numbered. As soon as this situation was contained tonight he would order the most hardened Special Forces teams to execute every last one of them. Excuses and explanation for their deaths could come later. Right now, this was a matter of survival. It was either them or him, and he knew it wasn't going to be him.

And yet in his heart, he harbored a deep, grim doubt about his ability to have such an order carried out. Not that he would ever admit it to anyone else, but Brooke had proved a serious adversary over the last few weeks. In fact, his resilience had surprised him. Now, after tonight, it was starting to frighten him. Brooke’s determination to take back the crown he had stolen from his head seemed unstoppable.

Much of that was down to ECHO. He knew from intelligence briefings back when he was Vice President that ECHO were generally assessed by security forces around the world as one of the most unpredictable and dangerous special ops teams in the world. He had doubted it at first, but now he was having fewer doubts. After tonight, it was starting to dawn on him that he had massively underestimated the ragtag team of international misfits, but he was determined not to let it be his downfall.

"We're ready to go, sir."

It was Muston. The young Chief-of-Staff was sitting opposite him in the surprisingly cramped interior of the helicopter. He looked scared, and after what happened back in DC, he could hardly blame him.

"This place has been searched, right?" Faulkner asked nervously. "I mean, the entire retreat."

"Yes, sir," Muston said. "We have marines all over the place."

Faulkner nodded but did not feel particularly comforted. "And what about you?" he asked the woman sitting opposite them. "You're sure you can take them out if they come up here?"

"Yes sir, Mr President," Agent Cougar said. "As soon as we land, you and Mr Muston will travel to the main compound. I will be going to another location in the woods, on elevated ground above the presidential residence and setting up the CheyTac there. If they get through the SAM missiles, they have to get past the marines roaming the grounds. If they get past the marines, they have to get past the US Secret Service agents around the residence. If they get past the Secret Service agents, then I'll take them out from hundreds of yards away. They're not getting to you tonight, sir. No way."

Listening to the confident and calm way she spoke and described the various defenses, Faulkner felt a little more persuaded he had a chance to survive the night and make revenge in the morning.

"Good," he said. "Get this right and you'll be heavily rewarded. Your boy will get the best care on Earth and you'll have the most comfortable retirement you ever dreamed of. Get it wrong, and I guess they'll bring you down before they even get to me."

"Relax," she said coolly. "With me, there is no wrong. There is no fail. I owe it to my son."

Faulkner showed a rare sign of humanity, leaning forward and patting her on the shoulder. "We're going to make it, Agent Cougar. All of us."

"We have to go, sir," Muston said as the chopper touched down.

On cue, a marine swung open the chopper's door and folded down the ladder. Then he turned and stood to attention outside the aircraft, bringing his right hand up in a crisp salute.

Faulkner stepped outside first, returning the salute with a slightly sloppier wave of his hand and then Muston and Cougar and a handful of suited officials climbed out and followed him along a path cut into the trees. At the end of it, they saw the lights of the main presidential residence, which was the most heavily fortified and guarded buildings in the entire retreat.

"Almost there, sir," Muston said, nervously glancing into the darkness of the forest on either side of the small party. "We're going to need to start talking about ending the threat posed by Brooke and ECHO once and for all."

"I'm already on it, Josh," Faulkner said. "Blaming them for the nukes was genius but just too goddamn complicated. Cougar here was too subtle. If they dare chase me here tonight then they will die in these mountains. If they stay away to regroup, we're going to need some serious wetwork to eliminate the whole lot of them."

"Yes, sir. We should have done that right from the start."

Faulkner stopped suddenly in the middle of the woods and stared at his Chief-of-Staff. "As I recall, Josh, it was *you* who first suggested we build on the Hawaii attack and frame them for the three nukes."

Muston swallowed hard, not enjoying the look in his boss's eyes. "Yes, sir. I thought it was a great way to take them all out once and for all. Getting you a solid rise in the polls after such an atrocity would be a great bonus, too."

Faulkner resumed his march to the residence. "Let's get inside and start working on a plan to take Brooke and these assholes down forever."

*

The last job, Cougar thought. This was it. After tonight she would have all the money she needed to save her son and escape to a new life. Leave this place behind her forever and never look back. That was what all of this nightmare was about and nothing more. She didn't care about the names or backgrounds of her targets. They were just contracts to be honored. Tonight, she would wrap up the final few names on the list as they tried to kill the president in his rural retreat. Nothing could be easier.

She had already found her sniping location – a small ridge to the east of the president's private residence – and was ready to go. The CheyTac Intervention bolt-action sniper rifle was almost set up now and when she clicked the seven-round single-stack magazine into the body, she was all set. Just another job. Another contract. Get it out of the way and pick up the paycheck and then she could be on her way. Back to LA to pay for Matty's operation and when he was recovering, the two of them would fly down to Justin in Los Cabos and buy her dream villa.

She could see it now. White stucco plaster reflecting the bright Mexican sun. Stepping out of her bedroom onto a varnished wooden deck and slipping into an infinity pool for a sunset dip while Justin and Matty cooked up some lobster on the barbecue. She heard the cicadas chirping and the sound of a maritime engine as a motorboat cut through the surf out in the Pacific. Her son laughing as Justin played the fool with the barbecue tongs.

A deep roar pulled her back to reality. The dream was gone. She was surrounded by the black woods of northern Maryland and somewhere behind her something had just met its maker. Turning, her slightly elevated position allowed her to see a missile roaring above the trees south of her position. She guessed the marines had just lit up the defensive missile battery situated out there. ECHO were obviously closer than they had thought – maybe even inside the perimeter. A tough, if not impossible job to most people, but she had watched these guys work over the last few weeks and wasn't as surprised as most would be around here tonight. In a fair fight, ECHO were practically impossible to beat.

Luckily, she didn't fight fair.

CHAPTER THIRTY-SIX

After exiting the White House the way they had come in, General Mulkey had been as good as his word and delivered the aircraft they needed to pursue the fleeing president and managed to source some extra muscle as well. Now, Lea Donovan looked at the team of Deltas opposite her on board the transport helicopter and prayed they would be enough to overcome Faulkner's forces up at Camp David.

These men were all loyal to Jack Brooke, himself a former Delta, and would fight to the death in order to unseat the usurper Faulkner, but there were only four of them. Combined with ECHO and Kahlia, Ravi and Tawan, that meant a force of just fourteen combatants. Brooke had told her to expect at least three times that many marines, plus US Secret Service Agents. All of a sudden, she didn't like the odds.

Hawke seemed less fazed by the math. He was leaning back in his seat and regaling one of the Deltas with an old war story from Afghanistan. Lots of hand movements and an occasional explosion sound from his mouth was met with a laugh from the grizzled American sergeant. Old lads recounting their bravery in great detail, but trying to make their daring exploits look modest at the same time.

Men, she thought with an eyeroll.

Then, the comms buzzed to life. "Incoming!"

It was the pilot and he sounded tense. She gripped the side of her seat as the chopper lurched violently to the right. A flash outside the window caught her attention. She spun her head just in time to see a missile streaking past the chopper at the head of a twisting column of smoke. The white exhaust trail flashed green in the helicopter's starboard position light but the warhead was long gone. She felt like screaming, but Kahlia did it for her instead.

Even Hawke looked nervous. "That was close."

"And it's not over yet!" said the pilot. "Hold on!"

This time, the chopper climbed and banked sharply to port to avoid a second missile, throwing Ravi from his seat and onto the floor. Some of the Deltas chuckled, but one of them held out his hand and pulled the Brazilian to his feet. "Hold on next time, friend."

Ravi smiled awkwardly. "I'll try and remember."

"I thought your guys were taking out the missile batteries?" the co-pilot called out over the comms. "We can't take too many more of these missiles. The stress of these turns is damaging the fuselage."

"They're on it," Lea said.

"Unless they already got killed..." said Lexi.

"Don't even think it, Lex," said Lea. "They're on it. I know they are. I'll check in with them and see what's going on."

When she spoke into the comms and listened for a response from Scarlet's team, she knew instantly that they had a problem. "They jammed all our comms."

"Predictable," Hawke said. "But we have a contingency. Cairo knows what to do."

*

Reaper and Scarlet made their way through the forest silently but fast. They each wore night vision goggles and carried sidearms and combat knives. They had travelled down on the same helicopter as the rest of the ECHO team but then they had been dropped off just north of the retreat before the chopper had gone on its way.

It was all part of the plan.

Now, they waited patiently just outside the perimeter for the transport helicopter to reappear. Seeing ECHO's helicopter arrive from the north, they prepared to break through the retreat's compound and take out the missile battery. Then, a flash from the trees and they both watched in horror as a missile streaked toward the chopper.

"Holy crap!" Scarlet said. "It looks on target, Reap."

"They're taking evasive action!"

"If only we could speak to them," she muttered.

"We knew they'd use a signal jammer, Cairo," Reaper said. "It's standard protocol."

For a few heart-stopping seconds, the two friends watched as the helicopter transporting their friends and the Deltas into the compound banked hard to starboard and avoided the missile. Then, another of the lethal projectiles fired into the sky and raced through the misty night sky toward the chopper. Another sharp lurch as it tipped almost on its side, this time to the left. The engine growled horribly in the darkness above them.

"They can't keep that up for long," Reaper said. "We have to take out the battery, maintenant!"

They scaled the fence and sprinted through the trees, branches scratching at them as they made their way deeper into the compound. Ahead, they saw the missile battery. It was a simple SAM setup manned by three marines. They both knew what to do and advanced in silence on the men guarding the battery. When they could get no further without giving themselves away, they sprang to life and darted out of the darkness of the surrounding trees.

Reaper piled into the two men standing guard nearer the trees and Scarlet slipped past them and charged the marine manning the battery. The attack soon exploded into a ferocious display of hand-to-hand combat as the two covert ops ECHO teammates grappled with the marines. With the sound of the Foreign Legionnaire's massive shovel fists crunching into the nose of one of the young marines behind her, Scarlet engaged with the man beside the SAM launcher.

Seconds later, her world had degenerated into a vicious battle for survival as the much bigger man tackled her to the ground. They rolled in the mud and leaves and she reacted like lightning to avoid the punches he was aiming at her head. Then one of them caught the side of her face and cut her cheek.

She cried out, more in surprise than pain. Surprise that she hadn't been fast enough to evade the blows. There was a time when that simply never happened, even with much faster opponents than this guy. She had to face the reality she was getting older just like everyone else, and now she'd have the scar to remind her for the rest of her life.

The pain from the gouge mark became more obvious and she didn't want another one. She forced him off her but he used his superior weight to roll again, positioning himself above her a second time and pinning her to the ground with a chokehold around her throat. With the vice grip on her windpipe, Scarlet knew her time was running out, so she brought her right knee up with all the force she could muster and crunched it into his lovemaking department. The blow from the impact had an immediate effect. He howled in agony and instinctively rolled away from her to bring his hands up to the damage.

As he curled up and grunted in pain, she sprang to her feet and aimed a kick at his face. Dimly aware that Reaper had knocked one guy out and was now moving onto the second man, she launched her boot into her opponent's sobbing face and knocked him out cold and clean. She wasted no time and spun around to help Reaper, but there was no need. By the time she had run over to his position he had already dispatched the final marine with an eye-watering cross-punch that landed directly in the middle of his face.

"Bloody hell, Reap," she said. "Are you sure you hit him hard enough?"

He shrugged. "It wasn't so bad."

"Not so bad? By the time he wakes up his clothes are going to be out of fashion."

He gave his Gallic shrug and winked at her. "He's wearing a uniform. They're never out of fashion."

As they took a fuel can from the back of the marines' Jeep and slopped it over the missile battery, she smirked at his attitude, and when he looked at her in the darkness of the forest, she was struck by a feeling she had never felt before. Not for him, at least.

"What is it?" he asked, casually tossing a match onto the battery and igniting it.

"Nothing," she said. "Just thinking about what an ugly, old bastard you are."

He gave a nonchalant nod. "The Renos of my hometown are famous for that, but we call it rugged, not ugly."

"Let's get out of here, Rugged," she said. "Joe's team will be landing about now and we don't want to miss the fun."

*

With the glow of the burning missile battery flickering in the forest below them, Lea gazed out of the small window as the chopper came into land. The few buildings that made up the retreat were separated by a good distance from one another and mostly tucked away in small pockets cut out of the forested hillside. Cosy in peacetime, but lethal tonight.

"All ready to go?"

She turned and saw Hawke. As ever, he seemed relaxed and was even offering a vague smile.

"I want this thing over, Joe. Tonight."

"And it's going to be."

As she climbed out of the chopper, she was relieved to see the black figures of Scarlet and Reaper bobbing out of the trees. Moments later they were together again. "All good?" she asked them.

Scarlet nodded. "Good and ready to finish this."

"We all are," Ryan said. Behind him the four Deltas were checking their weapons and comms. "It's time to go home now, back to Elysium."

And they started by fanning out and advancing through the trees toward the main residence to the north of the landing site. They didn't get far before the onslaught began. First, the sound of sidearms fire and then a heavy machinegun firing tracer rounds into the trees.

"Down!" Lea yelled.

Wherever they were standing, the team members dropped to the forest floor. Guns in hand and bated breath, they kept their heads down as the tracer fire lit up the surrounding woods and revealed their positions. Ryan stuck his head up to scan for the enemy when Alex saw a soldier take a pot shot at him. Without thinking, she crashed into him and knocked him to the ground as the bullet traced through the air where his head had been only moments earlier.

"Sodding hell that was close!" he said, looking into her eyes.

"Now we're even, I guess," she said with a shrug.

"Yeah," he said, reaching out and giving her arm a squeeze. "I suppose we are."

"These guys are good," Zeke called out, behind him, the Deltas returned fire, taking out some of the men near an outbuilding.

"Meh," said Hawke, trying to calm her nerves. "We can do better."

"I hope so, Hawke," Brooke said. "Because I know just how good these guys really are."

"Yeah, but we have to get forward," Hawke said. "We need to take out that machinegun nest."

"That's the main problem," Nikolai muttered. "If we can take that out, there's nothing else stopping us from going all the way in."

Hawke shook his head. "They're too well covered."

Then, Nikolai broke cover and sprinted through the trees toward the nest.

"No!" Hawke yelled. "Not like that!"

"I can take them out!" the Russian called back. "I can do it for the team!"

The bullet that killed him came not from the big, ugly general purpose machinegun parked outside the main residence, but from somewhere off to his right. Hawke watched in horror as a heavy duty, large round ripped the back of his friend's head off and sent his dead body tumbling to the ground. It rolled in the dust and leaves a few times before coming to a dreadful, grisly stop at the base of a tree trunk.

"Holy Mother of God!" Zeke called out. "The Secret Service killed Kolya!"

"No," Hawke said, his voice ice cold. "The bullet came from somewhere to the right, way off in the trees up on that elevation somewhere. I think it was the sniper."

His words almost froze time. With the sound of enemy fire zipping over their heads, the rest of the team realized the gravity of what Hawke had just said.

"It can't be!" Alex said. "Damn it, it just can't be!"

"Poor Kolya," said Zeke. "Damn all this to hell."

"We can't stop or mourn," Hawke said flatly. "We're here for a reason and we get on with it."

"But hell!" said the Texan. "Not Kolya! No way!"

"Yes way," Lea said, ducking down to avoid more incoming fire. "That bastard sniper was waiting for us in a concealed position… just waiting patiently for us to attack the residence."

In the chaotic, bullet-riddled darkness, Scarlet's eyes flashed like black diamonds as Camacho's death loomed darkly in her mind. "Then that bastard has come here tonight to die." Her voice was cold steel. "He's mine, Joe. And no one here had better try to stop me."

Lea felt the rage in her friend's voice. The brutal murder of Jack Camacho was still raw in everyone's mind and heart. She could only imagine how much worse it was for Scarlet. She only had to think about the sniper killing Hawke to get an idea of how she must be feeling. Now, with Nikolai added to his hitlist, things just got even worse.

Another short exchange of fire lit up the night. They all heard men screaming orders from just inside the residence. "All right, Cairo," Lea said. "There's no point trying to talk you out of it. I know you too well."

Scarlet looked at Nikolai's dead body and her mouth tightened. "Then I'm gone."

"Sure, but you're taking someone with you," the Irishwoman said.

"Reaper," Scarlet said without hesitation. "I want Reaper."

The Frenchman was already on his feet and crouch-walking through the mayhem toward Scarlet. Black beanie pulled low down on his forehead. When he spoke, the silver stubble on his chin caught the broken moonlight. “I’m ready when you are, Cairo.”

“We’re out of here, Lea,” Scarlet said. “We’ll take that cowardly, son of a bitch sniper out of the game for good while you guys get in there and end Faulkner.”

“That’s the plan, Cairo,” Hawke said, gun gripped in his hand. “Just take it easy. Don’t forget you’re a professional.”

“Yeah,” she said coolly. “A professional bitch.”

And then they were gone into the night.

CHAPTER THIRTY-SEVEN

Davis Faulkner felt the like the sand had almost reached the bottom of the hourglass. Here he stood, in the president's inner sanctum, surrounded by Secret Service agents and Marines specially selected for their loyalty, but he still couldn't shake off the feeling that time was running out. Even here, in the camp's underground situation room, he was beginning to get the idea that the game might be up.

Just minutes ago, one of his military commanders had informed him that the ECHO team had broken into two sub-units. One team had taken out the defensive missile battery and the other had abseiled out of a chopper near the south perimeter. Now, he turned a confused face to his Chief of Staff and for the first time in his life, didn't know what to say.

"We still have Krios, sir."

He looked up, almost startled to hear Muston's voice and he looked even more nervous than usual.

When Faulkner spoke, his words were thin and dry. "Yes, we have Krios."

Krios, one of the older Titans, was the father of Perses, the Titan god of destruction. Only tonight that wasn't what Krios meant. Tonight, Krios was not the name of an ancient deity but the designation of an aerial hydrogen bomb and the most powerful nuclear weapon ever created by man. Just thinking about it made Faulkner feel physically uncomfortable.

"It'll make the three mini-nukes we placed in the cities look like pea-shooters, Mr President."

This time the voice belonged to General Bill McAfee, an old-school warhorse with icy eyes and a face like welder's bench. He had supported Faulkner from the very start, decades ago.

"Pea-shooters?" Muston said. "Each one of those suitcase nukes would have killed hundreds of thousands of people, General."

"That's nothing compared to Krios, Mr Muston," McAfee said. "Krios is twice as powerful as the Tsar Bomba detonated by the Soviets back in 1961. It should yield at least one hundred megatons and give a blast radius of at least five miles."

"Meaning Washington DC will be wiped off the map for the rest of history," Muston said grimly. After a long, bleak pause, he added, "No… just no. We must rethink this. We can't do it. We can't be the men responsible for destroying the nation's capital. The Washington Monument, the Jefferson Memorial, the Capitol Building… the White House. All gone, incinerated along with millions of innocent lives."

"We'll do whatever the hell we have to!" Faulkner snapped. Like a cornered animal, he was starting to get very nasty. "Those bastards stopped the bombs in San Francisco, Chicago and New York. This is all that's left, Josh. If they get in here, they'll either arrest us or kill us. When you stop and think about the inevitable show trials and a life in Gitmo, death is the preferable option."

"The president is right," McAfee said grimly. "The only way we can save ourselves and stop this terrorist scum taking back control is to hit the reset button and take out all those traitorous bastards in DC. When Krios detonates, life as we know it is over. The president will declare it a terror attack on US soil by a band of treasonous terrorists led by Brooke and order emergency martial law with immediate effect. Then the military will be running the country from the Cheyenne Mountain Complex in Colorado."

Muston was horrified. "I thought we planned on the Mount Weather Emergency Operations Center in Virginia? At just over sixty miles away we can be there by chopper in minutes."

McAfee tried to contain his impatience with the young lawyer. "That's fine in most circumstances, Mr Muston, but not when you're going to detonate a one hundred megaton bomb on DC. It's too close. We'll be in danger of radioactive contamination."

"Like the millions of people living around DC, you mean?" Muston said.

Faulkner and McAfee both stared at him.

"You sound like you're losing your nerve, Mr Muston," McAfee said.

"No, but…"

Faulkner got up from his desk and wrapped an arm around Muston's shoulder. "Josh would never let me down, General. We've been through too much together, right Josh?"

After a short pause, Muston replied. "Yes, sir…we sure have been through a lot together."

"And you're as guilty as I am, Josh. Think about that."

Muston hesitated as the words sunk in. "You can count on me, sir."

"Good, because you know how I feel about traitors, right?"

On cue, General McAfee pulled back his army dress jacket to reveal the grip of a holstered SIG SAUER P320-M18. Nothing more had to be said.

Muston saw the weapon and swallowed hard. "Yes, sir. I'm as loyal as they come."

The phone rang, startling Muston and almost making him jump out of his skin.

McAfee snatched it up. "McAfee speaking. Go ahead."

Muston and Faulkner watched the General's face drop, then he replaced the receiver and turned to face his Commander-in-Chief, grim-faced. "That was Major Harding up top, sir. They've breeched the final perimeter and are almost inside the residence. We only have minutes left. We have to go now."

*

Agent Cougar ejected the empty case and blew out a long, slow breath. That was another one down – maybe the Russian monk, but she wasn't sure. It didn't matter anymore. All that mattered was one of the ECHO team had broken cover and was on his way to kill the president and she had stopped him with a round right through the head. Just work, nothing personal.

She got to her feet and moved fifty yards to her right. Never keep the same position after a fatal shot, Jessica, she told herself. Never give your position away. She slid another round inside the chamber and shook her shoulders loose. Cricked her neck and blew out another long breath.

Los Cabos.

Villa.

Justin.

Matty.

Hold it down, Jess. Almost there.

Steadying her hands, she gazed down through the sights and gently swept the weapon's terrifying barrel from side to side as she scanned the bedlam unfolding below. The president's residence was exploding into a raging barrage of gunfire as the Secret Service agents fought like hell to keep the terrorists away from the Commander in Chief. The only problem was the ECHO team were staying out of sight. Only one had so far been sloppy enough to get caught out in the wild. The rest were playing by more careful rules, but they would have to break cover and go inside the residence sooner or later.

Then she would strike. She preferred isolated, single shots but tonight she would have to work faster. Still, she reckoned she could take out at least three before they got into the cover of the residence – and that was supposing they even got that far. The men and women guarding the president were no joke, after all.

Then she saw what she had been waiting for. One of the ECHO team had broken cover and was running from the trees toward the machinegun nest. It was hard to say which one it was, but she thought maybe the Texan. Like the Russian, he was wearing mostly black fatigues and had obscured his face with camo grease.

Not anywhere near enough to save your ass, boy.

He was carrying a handgun and was now almost halfway to the machinegun nest. The rest of the team had been firing on another area to the right – an obvious piece of cover fire from ECHO designed to give them something to think about while the Texan charged their position. One eye gently closed, the other reduced to a narrow slit, she slowed her breathing and swept the barrel over to the target. Crosshairs lined up on the back of his head. Finger wrapped around the trigger.

A gentle squeeze, and…

A twigged snapped somewhere behind her. She gasped and spun her head around just in time to see Scarlet Sloane's gloved fist piling into the side of her head.

CHAPTER THIRTY-EIGHT

Another hefty explosion rocked the residence above their heads. "The General's right, sir. We have to get you out of here, right now," Muston said. "We thought you would be safe here but we were wrong. ECHO have got through every defensive line. They'll be down here in minutes."

"But go where?" Faulkner said.

"To the Raven Rock Mountain Complex," McAfee said. "Site R is close and easy to reach and it's a secure US military installation with a significant underground nuclear bunker complex. We'll be safe there, both from ECHO and Krios. As I recall, Raven Rock was my first suggestion but Mr Muston here persuaded us to come here."

Faulkner's eyes narrowed. "That's as may be, General, but we can't get to the chopper to get out to Raven Rock! They're all over the place like goddam ants! Like angry hornets! They'll cut us to shreds before we get halfway to any goddam chopper, and that's supposing there are any left up there still in a condition to fly!"

"There's a tunnel," McAfee said quietly. "A tunnel between Camp David and Site R."

Muston was astonished. "But it's six miles away!"

"Yes, but there's still a tunnel. It was originally built to contain comms cables in the event of a nuclear war, but it's big enough to use for personnel movements. We use specially adapted golf carts to move between the three locations."

Faulkner ran a hand through his hair, astonished and relieved. "Three locations?"

"It's a dog-leg tunnel running past Fort Richie, Mr President."

Suddenly, Davis Faulkner began to see his world coming back into focus. "A tunnel linking Fort Richie, Raven Rock and Camp David… I see. And how do we access this tunnel?"

"Right through here, sir," McAfee said. "The access door is in the anteroom to your personal quarters right next to this situation room."

"Who knows about it?"

"No one except key military personnel working here at the facility. Not even all ex-presidents know about it. We only tell them if they need to know. Tonight, you need to know."

After a few moments thought, a devilish smirk appeared on Faulkner's face. "Good work, General. Josh and I will take some Secret Service agents and drive over to Raven Rock. I want you to take a team of Marines and fly the Krios bomb over to DC."

"Yes sir, Mr President!"

Muston paled, but before he could speak, Faulkner said, "And listen to me very carefully, General McAfee. You are *not* and I repeat, *not*, to drop that weapon over DC until I give you the express order to do so. Is that clear?"

"Of course, sir."

"You won't survive the blast, General, " Muston said.

McAfee looked at him like he was crazy. "You think I don't know that, son? What I do tonight, I do for the survival of the republic. Now, it's time for us to move out. We need to go and we need to go now. It's time for exfil."

Faulkner didn't hang around to question the matter. He was already on his feet and making his way over to the tunnel's entrance. Beside him, the burly General McAfee growled like a bear ready for a fight. "Let's get out of here, gentlemen. We cannot let these terrorists take the president."

Faulkner readily agreed and ordered Josh Muston and some Secret Service agents into the tunnel. He felt a momentary wave of relief as they made their way down the cold concrete steps, but doubt fell over him like a shadow on a summer's day. He wasn't sure what it was, but something still told him he might just have seen his last sunrise.

*

Scarlet watched the woman roll away from a very serious sniping rifle and come to a stop a few feet away. Her face was bleeding from the blow she had landed on her temple but she was still conscious and now she scrambled to her feet and reached for a sidearm on a hip holster.

"Leave it!" Scarlet said coldly. "And get your hands nice and high."

The woman obeyed. Her shoulders sloped as she let out a long, nervous sigh. "Looks like you got me at last."

"Wait a minute," Scarlet said. "*You're* the sniper?"

Cougar nodded. "Yes I am."

Scarlet's eyes hardened. "You're the person who hunted us all over the world?"

"You look shocked," she said calmly. "Is it because I'm not a man?"

"It's because you killed so many of our friends."

"It was a job."

"Fuck your job," Scarlet shouted, startling even Reaper. "You killed my boyfriend."

Cougar played it cool. "You take no prisoners, I take it?"

"No prisoners, and no shit. Say goodnight, bitch, because you're about to be gone like yesterday." Scarlet raised her gun a little higher and aimed right between Cougar's eyes.

The young American woman had nothing to lose. She would rather risk a bullet in her arm or even her back than right through her forehead. She reacted like a wildcat and dived to the forest floor, rolling into the cover of some bushes.

A cursing Scarlet Sloane responded like lightning, emptying her entire magazine all over the last place she had seen her, the muzzle flashes lighting up the rage on her face as she fired. Reaper ran forward, covering her with his own gun, aware she had emptied her mag all over the fleeing woman. But now Scarlet was already kicking at the bushes in search of her prey.

"She got away, Reap!"

"No, I see her. She's running down a track toward the residence. She's trying to get to safety, somewhere with more of her own side. Safety in numbers."

"Not tonight." Scarlet scrambled through the bushes and ran down the tree-flanked path until she saw the woman sprinting away. The clouds broke once again and allowed the moonlight to briefly illuminate the fleeing assassin. She raised her gun as Cougar continued running for the main compound and showed her no mercy. This was the woman who had killed Devlin and Lund and Kim and Nikolai.

And Jack Camacho.

Raising her gun into the aim, Scarlet fired a short but deadly burst of rounds into the sniper's back and knocked her violently to the muddy floor. She crashed down hard, her bullet-riddled body now leaking blood all over the path running from the woods to the president's residence.

"The bitch has gone, Reap," she said into her palm mic.

"And when you say gone…" Reaper said.

“Dead as a doornail, Vincent. I used her arse for target practice.”

“No more than the bitch deserved,” he said quietly.

“Yeah, and there’s more.”

“What?”

“A helicopter is taking off from the north side of the residence. Marine One, I think. Maybe it’s Faulkner. I’m not sure, but whoever it is has some marines in tow.”

“I can see it through the windows of the residence,” Hawke said, his voice weak over the comms. “It’s not Faulkner. It’s one of the generals and he looks pretty grim. Lea just radioed in from the lower level. Faulkner’s gone down into some kind of escape tunnel again. You get inside here and give Lea some backup and leave the chopper to me.”

CHAPTER THIRTY-NINE

Already one hundred feet over the forest canopy and Marine One's wheels were retracting inside the undercarriage bay. All good, except that Hawke was gripping hold of the VH-92A's portside wheel's support strut assembly when it happened. Hydraulics whined in his ears and the rainstorm lashed at his face as he gripped hold of the side float above the assembly. He brought his right foot up and slammed it down on top of the wheel, then pushed himself up over the float housing.

Rain and wind still beating on his face, he walked up the fuselage-mounted sponson, searching the slippery metal hull for anything he could grab onto to secure himself. Up ahead, he saw the crew entrance. A thousand flights in this model told him this was a fold-down door with a fitted staircase on the inside. The other side of the chopper sported a sliding door, which would be easier but he was on this side, take it or leave it.

He estimated the chopper was at least a thousand feet now and starting to break through some low cloud. As it passed through the aerosol droplets, the helicopter rocked from side to side with turbulence. He'd anticipated it and increased his grip on a grab-handle on the fuselage. The juddering reduced when the chopper broke through the clouds but instead of seeing the tops of the clouds and a moon above him, he saw another layer of much higher rain clouds.

Flying in between the two layers in the rain, the aircraft made its way at full speed toward Washington DC. Calculating the chopper's top cruising speed and the distance from Camp David to the capital he worked out he had less than twenty minutes to get inside the cockpit, take out the pilot and regain control of the aircraft. He just prayed there were no more nasty surprises inside the aircraft.

Reaching the door's handle, he pulled on it and forced it down with all his might. The heavy metal door slowly opened and swung down to reveal a series of steps leading inside the helicopter's main cabin. He had a two-foot jump to make from the side float sponson to the bottom step and nothing much to grab hold of if he slipped.

Who Dares Wins, as Scarlet would probably say.

A face appeared in the darkness of the cabin's interior. It was a marine, shocked to see a man trying to climb inside the chopper hundreds of feet above the ground. He drew a gun, but Hawke was faster, swinging his pistol up into the aim at arm's length and firing three shots into his chest.

The marine tumbled out of the helicopter door and spun down through the clouds and mist below. Hawke saw another marine appear in the door, this time holding an automatic rifle. He swung it up and aimed at him but before he got a shot off, Hawke smacked the muzzle to the side and piled into him, pushing him back inside and into another marine standing behind him.

The chopper rocked in heavy turbulence, knocking all three men to the side and nearly off their feet. They scrambled to right their balance but Hawke was fastest. He headbutted the first marine and snatched his weapon from him, then opened fire in the tiny cabin, drilling them both with holes. One was killed outright but the other had survived for long enough to draw a sidearm and fire on Hawke.

The Englishman had nowhere to run except back out of the door. He leaped outside and fell from the chopper, only just grabbing the float in time to stop himself from falling all the way to the ground. Gun still in his hand, he fired on the surviving marine while dangling from the bottom of the chopper, striking him several times in the chest and finishing the job. As the blood-soaked marine fell to the helicopter's carpet, Hawke pulled himself back up to the top of the float. He had to make the jump over to the door again.

Deep breath and a leap into the rainy darkness. He flew through the air, above him the chunky whine of the main rotors whirring above his head. His right foot crashed down on the wet bottom step and skidded off the end. He tipped backwards but grabbed hold of the flimsy metal handrail, saving himself for long enough to swing his left leg around and slam his foot down on the next step up.

Up the steps and into the cabin, he looked past the dead marines and saw a hideous, black tic-tac shaped object with a large steel caisson at one end protecting a substantial tail fin assembly. Everything was bolted together with big, ugly metal rivets but luckily he saw no countdown timer. Then he saw what looked like an artillery fuse on board and guessed he was looking at a time-of-fall fuse, to be set when the thing was almost ready to go.

Thank heavens for small mercies, he thought.

And then he turned into the cockpit where he now saw the back of General McAfee's helmet-covered head as he piloted the aircraft down toward the bottom layer of cloud. They must be over the northern districts of Washington by now with probably less than a few minutes to reach the capitol's center. The sick bastard was going to turn the White House into some kind of Ground Zero.

Not on my watch, he muttered, and stepped into the cockpit.

*

Lea Donovan raced the golf cart along the final few yards of the white-painted concrete tunnel leading to Raven Rock. She worried about Hawke but he was out of range and out of contact and she had to put him out of her mind. She was hunting a man who had already tried to detonate three nuclear bombs on US soil and God only knew what the hell was inside Marine One when it took off in such a hurry.

A man like Faulkner was capable of anything and right now they almost had him in a corner. One slip up and she was dead. They all were. She felt her past racing up behind her, ready to crash into whatever future lay ahead of her. They had already lost Kamala Banks and Nikolai Petrov. Whatever happened tonight, she couldn't let any more of her team come to harm. But she wasn't alone. While most of the team had stayed up top with the Deltas to guard the entrance to the tunnel, Reaper and Scarlet were at her side. They were comrades-in-arms, going way back together.

Turning the cart around the final corner, Scarlet saw it first. The golf cart Faulkner had used to escape from Camp David was rattling along the corridor toward a large concrete hub area filled with crates and doors and several other golf carts.

"There! Faulkner, Muston and two Secret Service agents!" Scarlet said. "They're getting out and heading for one of those doors!"

Lea saw it too. He wasn't getting away. Not today. Not anymore. This was their last chance and they all knew it. Up top in Raven Rock would be hundreds of armed soldiers who would follow the orders of their Commander-in-Chief and kill ECHO where they stood.

She swerved the cart to halt and a startled Faulkner turned around in horror. He pointed a trembling finger at them and screamed at the agents protecting him.

"Kill them! Kill them all!"

Lea was fast. Drawing her gun, she leaped from the cart and pointed her gun in the center of Faulkner's face.

"Nobody move!" she yelled.

Faulkner and Muston froze. Beside them, the two agents also froze in space, each with a hand on their holsters.

"Hands up nice and high," she said coolly. "Right now or he's dead."

They obeyed and a visibly shocked Faulkner took a step back.

"All right, what now?" he said.

"You know what now, Faulkner," Lea said.

"You can't win," he said calmly. "I've already ordered the detonation of the Krios."

"What's that?" Scarlet said.

He smiled. "It's the most powerful nuclear weapon ever made. It was originally built back in the seventies in a top secret program in response to the Soviet Union's Tsar Bomba. Only Krios is twice as powerful. Its blast radius is at least five miles in diameter. When it goes off, Washington DC is gone forever, along with the whole of Congress and any chance you have of legally removing me from power. I will declare martial law and have you arrested on the spot."

Lea was horrified by what she had just heard. Beside her, Scarlet and Reaper were both covering the two agents, a gun aimed firmly at each one as they waited for her to make her move. Muston had turned white and was trembling behind them, shaking hands high in the air.

"Where is this bomb?" Lea asked.

A feverish-looking Faulkner raised his chin defiantly. “Why should I tell you?”

Reaper took a step forward. Beside him, Scarlet said, “Don’t make him force it out of you, Faulkner. Two minutes with this guy and you’ll fall apart like a wet cake.”

Faulkner eyed the massive Frenchman. “Fine, you can’t do anything about it anyway. It’s on board a helicopter bound for the capital. It’s over, Donovan.”

She thought back to Hawke and Scarlet talking about the general getting on board Marine One and felt another wave of horror wash over her. She had to talk to Hawke, but first, the Faulkner Problem.

“What you did to us was unforgivable, Faulkner.”

He gave her a snarl and an insolent shrug. “You’re criminals. What happened to you was a long time coming. When I got into office, you just ran out of luck. That’s all.”

She squeezed her gun tighter. “And you just ran out of road.”

“I don’t think so!” Faulkner screamed, and surprised her by reaching into his own jacket and pulling an automatic pistol. In a heartbeat, he had lifted it into the aim and was pointing it at her face. “Goodnight, ECHO!”

CHAPTER FORTY

Hawke and McAfee realized two different things at the same time. The old USAF general saw movement in the reflection of the cockpit glass, and Hawke knew he'd been rumbled. As McAfee reached for his sidearm, Hawke leaped into the cockpit and grabbed his left shoulder. Pulling him roughly back away from the controls, he threw his arm out and smacked the service pistol from his grip. It clanged on the metal floor in front of the pilot's seat, but McAfee was ready with his reply, thrusting his helmeted head back and smashing Hawke in the face with it.

The Englishman stumbled back with a blood-streaked face and nearly fell over, only just stopping himself by grabbing hold of the back of the pilot's chair. McAfee fumbled with his safety harness. He wanted up and out of his seat so he could attack Hawke again, but the old commando was a step ahead and kicked out with his right leg, landing his combat boot squarely in the old man's face and smashing him back against the controls.

"No!" Hawke yelled.

It was too late. McAfee had already staggered back and crunched his boot down on the collective, sending the massive helicopter down into the clouds. Hawke grabbed a fistful of his dress jacket and drove a bone-crunching headbutt into the middle of his face. The old man cried out in pain but Hawke had already powered a hefty punch right under his ribs and knocked the wind out of his lungs.

Coughing and grunting in agony, McAfee was learning about fighting a much younger man with commando training. Hawke now reached up and pushed his thumb into his left eye socket, making him scream out like a child. Now, the English Special Ops man pistol whipped him with his left hand but he still fought back. Hawke had no choice, and now pushed his gun up under his ribs and fired four shots, killing him instantly. Heaving him out of the seat, Hawke leaped down in front of the flight controls just in time to see the ground racing up toward him.

The aircraft whined and howled as he pulled back on the controls, desperately trying to pull out of the nosedive. With seconds to spare, the helicopter levelled off a few feet above the streets of Washington below, ripping and biting at the tops of suburban trees until Hawke was able to power up and gain some elevation.

Wiping sweat from his forehead, he blew out a deep breath and prepared to turn the chopper back when he heard a loud electronic bleeping noise. He twisted around in the pilot's seat and saw a red glow coming from the cabin's interior. Scrambling out of the seat, he ran over to the bomb and saw a timer had been activated. The countdown said thirty minutes.

"Christ on a bike," he mumbled, taking in the massive bomb with the glowing timer. "I don't know exactly what you are, but you look bad."

*

When Lea pulled the trigger, she kept her finger wrapped tight around it until she had emptied the entire magazine into Davis Faulkner. The gun was blasted from his hand, and each bullet that tore into him was bloody payback for all the torture he had meted out on them, for all the people they cared about that this monster had killed.

The agents reached for their guns, but Scarlet and Reaper cut them down before their hands got anywhere near the steel grips of the weapons. Muston screamed and turned toward the door but was cut down in the crossfire.

Lea saw none of it. She was focusing only on the man in her own crosshairs. Faulkner. As the rounds chewed into him, his bullet-riddled body jerked from side to side with their impact until he finally crashed to the ground. Only when she was standing over his smoking, blood-soaked corpse and saw his dead, glazed eyes, did she know it was finally over.

And then, she cried.

*

Hawke ran back into the cockpit and this time saw the timer activation control in McAfee's right hand. The old bastard had triggered it just before he'd killed him. He jumped down into the pilot's seat and reached for his cell phone, but before he got it up to his ear, it rang.

Lea.

"Joe!"

"Lea – what's up with Faulkner?"

"Faulkner has been blackbagged," he heard Scarlet say.

Lea sighed. "Faulkner's dead but forget about that! You need to know something."

"Don't tell me – there's a bomb on this helicopter?"

"You saw it?"

"Uh-huh. Looks nasty."

She explained what it was. "All you have to do is turn the chopper around and get back here to Raven Rock. Then we can work out what to do with it. Ryan can deactivate it, I know he can."

"Yeah, about that plan." Hawke sighed. "Did I tell you it was on a thirty minute timer?"

"Bollocks. Where are you now?"

"Past DC. No way can I get it back to Raven Rock in time and with a blast radius like that it's going to cause total devastation if it goes off anywhere on land. I have to get it out to sea."

"Bloody hell, Joe! What about you?"

"Well, it's not a suicide mission, that's for sure. No way am I going to ride this bomb all the way to the ground! So I need you to listen carefully. Alert all maritime traffic to immediately vacate the eastern seaboard off the coast of Delaware. You can track the chopper via the transponder and me via the cell phone GPS."

"And?"

"And leave the rest to me. But don't forget to get Mulkey to send a sea rescue chopper out. It's cold out here tonight and I won't last long."

"Joe! This is crazy… you can't just…"

Already flying over the Delaware coast, he cut the call and got to work. Flying the chopper down to almost sea level, he then set the autopilot – a new function on the very latest VH-92s – to maintain the current low altitude and keep a heading of ninety degrees. He set speed for maximum cruise and then climbed up out of the seat. Leaping over McAfee's dead body, he saluted the bomb and leaped outside the door.

Diving out of helicopters at night into the ocean was standard training for Special Boat Service operatives, so the experience offered few surprises as the Englishman crashed into the North Atlantic and started praying they'd already located his cell phone signal before the seawater started working its magic. As he watched the chopper recede into the darkness of the ocean, he uttered another prayer that the new autopilot technology would work long enough to get Krios far enough away to ensure he was well outside the blast radius.

But he didn't have to wait long for help. Less than twenty minutes after he had jumped from Marine One, a sea rescue chopper roared over the western horizon, searchlights blazing. It hovered over his position for a few seconds and then a crewman lowered a rope outside the aircraft's main door. Hawke grabbed it and gave the signal to be brought back up. Inside, he shook hands with the crew, all loyal to General Mulkey and briefed them on the bomb.

They already knew all about it and the pilot was already turning in a tight arc and heading back to the coast. Then, thirty miles away on the Atlantic continental shelf, Krios detonated just above sea level. The sky behind them lit up like midday, an insane explosion of blinding, white-hot light that rapidly turned orange and red. Clouds were blasted from the sky and billions of tons of water blown up into the air before being instantly evaporated by the tremendous heat.

Through the comms, the pilot's voice was steady but slightly nervous. "Brace!"

Then the shockwave hit. Reduced in power by the vast distance it had to cover to reach them, it was still strong enough to rock the chopper savagely from side to side in the worst turbulence Hawke had ever known. At one point, he wondered if they would be able to stay airborne, but the pilot maintained control and levelled the aircraft off.

Hawke closed his eyes and said a quiet thanks to anyone who might be listening.

It was over.

CHAPTER FORTY-ONE

Sir Richard Eden rose from his chair and raised a glass. "And now a toast."

Among the ruins of Elysium, the rest of the ECHO team pushed back their chairs, stood and raised their glasses. They were standing around the long table in what had once been their plush conference room on the private Caribbean island.

With Faulkner gone forever they were safe to return here once more, but to say the place needed some TLC was the understatement of the century. Their old nemesis had ordered the place to be bombed back into the stone age and his pilots had clearly taken that order very seriously.

But others had it worse. The devastation from the Krios detonation was still being counted and assessed, with the NBC sniffer bird chopper still circling around Delaware testing the air quality. Thanks to Hawke's hard work, it seemed the radiation had gone mostly out into the ocean, but already Congress was commissioning a major investigation into it, including the biggest environmental assessment ever conducted by the US Government not to mention the enquiry in the Faulkner debacle.

Now, Eden looked at them one by one. "I wish I'd thought of something to say in advance now."

They all groaned. Scarlet downed her champagne and poured a second glass.

"Joking aside," Eden continued, "Last week, you did what you have done so many times before. You risked your lives to fight the good fight and do the right thing.

This time, you stopped a maniac from taking over the American government. You also saved my life and got me out of house arrest, but we didn't all come through it. We lost many of our closest friends and colleagues."

As he spoke the names of the fallen, a respectful hush descended on the blown out conference room. Two more fallen friends to add to the island's memorial garden. It didn't bear thinking about.

"And you can count me out too," Zeke said.

The others turned to him, shocked.

"Eh?" Hawke asked. "You're not leaving us, are you mate?"

"Sorry, but yes. My family need me back in Texas and I promised them some help. I helped you guys take out Faulkner and get started on the island, but now it's time for me to bid you guys farewell, at least for the time being. I hope that's all good."

"It's all good," Lea said. "You'll stay in touch?"

"Sure I will. And maybe I'll ride alongside you crazy bastards one more time."

In the sad silence, Eden paused and looked around at the ruins of their old HQ. The team had been here for nearly a week getting generators set up and clearing rubble, but he had only just arrived a few hours ago. "I can see you've already tried to pull some of the chaos together, but we're going to need some outside help to bring this place back to its former glory. It's going to take some serious manpower and heavy plant equipment to get the buildings back in shape and that's before we even start considering the electronic equipment."

"As long as we start with the bar and a couple of high quality fridges, I'm okay," Scarlet said, wincing as she downed her champagne and then sipped from a tall glass of warm bourbon. "Ice. There is no civilisation without ice."

"As someone who spent the last few months in Tartarus, I agree with all my heart," Kahlia said.

Beside her, Ravi laughed and gently squeezed her hand. "I agree, and I'm sure the venerable Tawan will also agree!"

"Tawan who?" said Eden.

Hawke chortled quietly and shook his head. "A real character, that's who."

"He's one of our new friends," Lea said. "We found him on Tartarus along with Kahlia and Ravi."

"Yes, I know," Eden said. "You told me in your message a few days ago. I meant Tawan *who*, as in, what's the rest of his name?"

Hawke grinned. "It's just Tawan. He's very good, though."

"He'd have to be to pull off the one-name thing," Eden said.

"I think you mean a mononymous person," said Ryan.

Scarlet snorted. "He meant what he said, fool."

"Mononymous?" Kahlia asked.

"Zeno, Boudica, Molière, Maradona, Madonna… and now Tawan."

"I don't believe I've had the pleasure of meeting this chap," Eden said. "Is he on the island now?"

"He sure is," Lea said. "Somewhere over on the west coast, meditating."

"What's his field?" Eden asked.

Kahlia said, "He's a Thai smuggler, ex-Thai special forces and *muay thai* expert with an impressive collection of Thai flying knives and he knows how to use them. And also, he's a pirate."

"A Thai pirate?" Lexi asked with one eye raised. "You're having some fun at our expense, right?"

"No."

"Why not ask him now?" Hawke said. "Like Lea said, he's been working on some of the buildings on the west of the compound and it looks like he's coming back for something to eat. He's over there – sprinting through the surf."

"Ah, surf," Kahlia said. "Give me surf over anything else."

Ravi slipped his arm around her. "Over *anything else*?"

"Fine, *almost* anything else, Senhor Monteiro," she said, leaning over to kiss him on the mouth.

Scarlet made a big show of an eye roll. "Please, I'd close my eyes but I can't be arsed. Can't you go somewhere else to carry on like that? You two are as bad as Alex and the boy."

Eden's ears pricked up. "Sorry, Alex and Ryan are together now?"

"Sickening, isn't it?" Scarlet said.

"Where is Alex?" Eden said, seeing she was the only member of the team not present.

"On a phone call," Lea said.

Eden smiled. "Well, how wonderful! Ryan and Alex!"

Scarlet rolled her eyes. "Apparently, they saved each other's lives at different times on the mission and now they're blathering on about kismet."

Eden smiled. "You're such a cynic, especially for someone who has only recently been struck by Cupid's arrow."

She glanced at Reaper and then blushed and shrank into her chair. "Vincent and I don't comment on our private lives," she said with a sly smile.

Reaper shrugged and lit a cigarette. "This is true, and don't look at me like that. I know there's a no smoking rule inside Elysium, but I refuse to obey such a rule in any room without a roof on it."

Lea laughed and took a sip of her champagne. Maybe the old times could come back after all.

"What a happy little family we are, then," Eden said. "Joe and Lea, Scarlet and Vincent, Alex and Ryan, Kahlia and Ravi. That just leaves you Lexi."

"And Tawan," Lea said with a coy smile aimed at the enigmatic assassin.

"No, that wouldn't work," Ryan said. "Tawan's a good bloke from what I've seen. Plus Lex is already in a long-term relationship with her own ego."

Lexi's eyes flashed. "Bite me, Bale."

Tawan stepped through the rubble and joined the group with a quiet nod. "Did someone say my name?"

"You don't want to know," Lexi said. "Believe me."

Another chuckle, but then Eden's face grew more serious. "If I might interject…"

"Please, can't you wait until you're alone?" Ryan said, raising a light titter.

"Very good, Mr Bale, but no. And this is serious. Following an earlier Zoom call that was cut off, I spoke on the flight from London to Elysium with a senior MI5 colleague of mine, and former Paras officer, Nigel Gambles. He contacted me because he had some unnerving chatter about King Kashala coming back on the scene. He's been tracking Kashala's smuggling operations for some time now and has suggested a joint operation with his team to capture the Congolese warlord."

"Blimey."

"And there's more. Another officer working in an MI6 office in Switzerland reported some even more unsettling news to Nigel."

Lea frowned. "What was it, Rich?"

"If I say the name Dietmar Grobel, what does it conjure up?"

"Poseidon!" Lea said in the stunned silence.

"Who, what, where, why and when?" said Kahlia.

"Dietmar Grobel was the right-hand man of a criminal mastermind called Hugo Zaugg," Eden said. "They were behind one of the most remarkable operations I've ever known. Nigel's agent in Zürich has now reported that Grobel was broken out of a prison in Zürich a few days ago by a professional team, probably ex Special Forces, maybe German maybe Russian."

"Bloody hell," Scarlet said. "I didn't see that coming."

"Quite," Eden said. "And it gets worse. Nigel believes the breakout was masterminded by a woman from Bern named Nina Zaugg, Hugo's daughter."

Silence.

"My sentiments exactly," Eden continued. "I'm not a fan of idle conjecturing, and we don't know if this means anything substantive at this stage, but it might be pointing toward something we need to keep an eye on. Hugo Zaugg and Poseidon was a serious business and maybe Grobel and Nina Zaugg have something planned."

"Which is why we need this place up and running as fast as possible," Hawke said. "With Kashala and Grobel on the loose, we need all our resources. And this Nina Zaugg is a totally unknown quantity. Ryan and Alex need to get on with the cyber end of things especially fast. We can't remain operational at this level without our full network up and running."

"Talk of the devil," Lea said as Alex walked into the room. She had her phone to her ear and was clearly at the end of a conversation. She slipped the phone away and realized everyone was staring at her. "Wait, what's up?"

"Cairo told Rich about you and Ryan," Lea said.

"Ah…"

Eden raised his glass of warm champagne. "And I couldn't be more happy for the two of you. Congratulations."

She tried to hide her smile. "Thanks, Rich."

"No more going to strip clubs now, boy," Scarlet said.

"I never go to strip clubs! I'm far too innocent."

"You sound a little too blasé to me," Alex said. "Like that sentence was just plucked out of your imagination rather than reality."

"Ya reckon?" he said.

"Uh-huh."

"But it's true!" Ryan protested. "Well, except for that time after the Lost City mission in Rio, when Joe took me into a club in Copacabana and started throwing money at the strippers."

"Oh yeah…" Hawke said, rapidly ending his smile when he saw the look on Lea's face. "That never happened."

"Oh yeah?" she said with an eyebrow raise.

He nodded. "I know it's rubbish because when I enter a strip club, the strippers throw money at *me*."

She slapped his arm. "Eejit."

Eden chuckled. "It's good to be back!"

Hawke turned to Alex, changing the subject. "What did they say on the call?"

"The money's there, all ready to go."

"Money?" Eden asked.

"After Dad got back into the Oval Office and set up the new cabinet, he unfroze ECHO's accounts and assets. I just transferred an amount for personal use, I hope that's all right."

"Personal use?"

Hawke spoke up. "At the end of the mission, President Brooke's new Chief of Staff Mike Mulkey sent Alex some information about the person sent to kill us… the sniper."

"And was it the Spider?" Eden asked, then paused. "Was it the man who killed your wife?"

Hawke shook his head. "No, the Spider, otherwise known as Alfredo Lazaro, was not the sniper. In fact it was a woman named Jessica Clarke, codename Agent Cougar. And she had a sick son."

Eden was shocked. "Bloody hell."

Ryan said, "And Cairo killed her at Camp David."

"Double bloody hell."

"Exactly, Lea said. "It turns out she took the contract to kill us to pay for her son's medical care. Some kind of operation that's very important to him. We don't know what. I took the decision to release the funds to pay for the operation. We killed his mother, after all."

"His mother was a psychopath who picked us off one by one," said Lexi.

"And her son is a little boy who is totally innocent," Lea said firmly. "We took his mother away, and now we're paying for the operation."

"Agreed," Eden said. "Do we know the doctor's name?"

"Amelia Fernandez."

"Good. Does the boy have any other family?"

"According to the intel report Mike gave Dad," Alex said, "Agent Cougar had a half-sister somewhere in New England that she never even knew about. They never even met, but she's blood family and she's already agreed to take the boy. Sadly, she can't afford the cost of the operation."

"Luckily, she doesn't have to," Eden said coolly. "How do we pay for it?"

"We can transfer it electronically," Ryan said.

"Yeah," Alex said. "It's no problem at all now Dad's back in the White House. Like I said, now all our assets are unfrozen we can do what we want. We could just make the payment."

"No," Scarlet said flatly. "I killed his mother. I'm taking the money."

*

Scarlet Sloane walked down the long, white corridor with a tatty, old carpet bag gripped in her right hand. She disliked places like this intensely. Sterile and chilly with the air-conditioning, it harbored a permanent smell of disinfectant in the air.

She turned and approached a large semi-circular desk. Several nurses were sitting behind it and two doctors were standing nearby, holding clipboards and chatting quietly to one another. Behind the nurses' station, she saw a room with the door ajar. Inside, lying on the bed, was a young boy she recognized from her briefing report as Jessica Clarke's son.

"I need to speak to Doctor Fernandez."

The nurse closest to her looked at up and gave an empty smile. "Do you have an appointment?"

"No."

"Then you can't speak with her."

One of the doctors turned and looked at her. "I'm Doctor Fernandez."

"And you're Matthew Clarke's doctor?"

"I can't divulge private and personal information unless…"

"Save it. The child is awaiting an operation, yes?"

The woman was visibly shocked. "Like I said, I'm not at liberty to discuss any further details with you."

"I'm giving you details, not asking for them." Scarlet lowered her voice. "I know you're trying to finalize details now with his mother's insurance company, but that's not going to happen. She had no insurance policy."

The doctor started to look more concerned. "What are you talking about?"

"His mother passed away in an accident on the East Coast so she can no longer pay for the operation and there isn't going to be any insurance money either. That's why I'm here, today."

The doctor now looked confused. "I'm sorry. Who are you, exactly?"

"A family friend. I'm here to pay for the operation." She hefted the bag up on the table between them. She opened it up and the doctor peered inside at the bundles of one hundred dollar bills. "There's more than enough money in here to cover it, I presume."

The doctor's eyes widened considerably. "Um, yes. I would think so. But this is pretty unorthodox."

"I don't care about any of that," the English aristocrat said coolly. "I don't do orthodox and I don't do admin. This is my money and I want to pay for his operation. You talk to your finance department and get it arranged. Get me a receipt if it makes you feel better. Then it's over."

"Why are you doing this?"

Scarlet peered through a door behind the station and looked at the young boy in the bed and fought back memories of her own childhood and the terrible night she watched her parents die. Then her mind fast-forwarded to a few hours ago when she killed Agent Cougar.

"Because it's the right thing to do."

THE END

AUTHOR'S NOTE

I hope you enjoyed coming along on this latest adventure with Hawke and the ECHO team. This is now the fifteenth Hawke novel and pivotal to the ECHO team's adventures. By way of refreshing the series and taking the stories in exciting new directions, Hawke and the rest of the team continue in a brand new and very different type of mission in *Gold Train* (Joe Hawke 16) in which the team must battle with a dangerous enemy from their past. I'm sure ECHO will rise to the unique challenge presented in this upcoming story with their usual style, panache and extreme violence!

Look out for news on this coming up soon as well as the subsequent release, *The Last Warlord* (Joe Hawke 17). I'll also be updating very soon with exciting news on the third instalment of the Hunter Files, *The Titanic Mystery*.

Stay safe in these troubled times, everyone & keep well.

Rob

JOE HAWKE WILL RETURN IN
GOLD TRAIN

Printed in Great Britain
by Amazon

59251509R00147